THE HEART OF A REBEL

*Legendary doctors
who aren't afraid to break the rules!*

**Mills & Boon® Medical™ Romance
brings you a brand-new trilogy
from favourite author Alison Roberts!**

*There'd been four of them once upon a
time. But, after the loss of their best friend,
now there is just Max, Rick and Jet. These
rebel doctors have formed an unbreakable
brotherhood—a bond that would see them
put their lives on the line for each other...*

Now these bad boys are about to be tamed!
But it'll take a special kind of woman
to see past their tough exteriors
and find the heart of a rebel...

This month meet Max
(THE HONOURABLE MAVERICK)
and Rick (THE UNSUNG HERO).

Then look out for Jet's story, coming soon!

The Heart of a Rebel

*Legendary doctors
who aren't afraid to break the rules!*

Dear Reader

OK. Personal confession time, here :-)

I'm one of those women who find certain tough, leather-clad men who ride powerful motorbikes irresistibly sexy.

Can this image be improved on?

I thought so. What if these men are also fabulously good-looking, highly intelligent, and capable of putting their lives on the line for the people they love?

For each other.

For children.

For their women.

These are my 'bad boys'. Max, Rick and Jet. Bonded by a shared tragedy in the past, but not barred from a future filled with love.

Enjoy.

I certainly did :-)

With love

Alison

THE
HONOURABLE
MAVERICK

BY
ALISON ROBERTS

First published in Great Britain 2011
by Mills & Boon, an imprint of Harlequin (UK) Limited.
Large Print edition 2011
Harlequin (UK) Limited, Eton House,
18-24 Paradise Road, Richmond, Surrey TW9 1SR

© Alison Roberts 2011

ISBN: 978 0 263 21766 7

Harlequin (UK) policy is to use papers that are natural, renewable and recyclable products and made from wood grown in sustainable forests. The logging and manufacturing process conform to the legal environmental regulations of the country of origin.

Printed and bound in Great Britain
by CPI Antony Rowe, Chippenham, Wiltshire

Alison Roberts lives in Christchurch, New Zealand. She began her working career as a primary school teacher, but now juggles available working hours between writing and active duty as an ambulance officer. Throwing in a large dose of parenting, housework, gardening and pet-minding keeps life busy, and teenage daughter Becky is responsible for an increasing number of days spent on equestrian pursuits. Finding time for everything can be a challenge, but the rewards make the effort more than worthwhile.

Recent titles by the same author:

ST PIRAN'S: THE BROODING
   HEART SURGEON†
THE MARRY-ME WISH*
WISHING FOR A MIRACLE*
NURSE, NANNY…BRIDE!
HOT-SHOT SURGEON, CINDERELLA BRIDE
THE ITALIAN SURGEON'S
   CHRISTMAS MIRACLE

†*St Piran's Hospital*
*Part of the *Baby Gift* collection

CHAPTER ONE

THE three men stood in close proximity.

Tall. Dark. Silent.

Clad in uniform black leather, motorbike helmets dangled from one hand. They each held an icy, uncapped bottle of lager in the other hand.

Moving as one, they raised the bottles and touched them together, the dull clink of glass a sombre note.

Speaking as one, their voices were equally sombre.

'To Matt,' was all they said.

They drank. A long swallow of amber liquid. Long and slow enough for each of them to reflect on the member of their group no longer with them. Cherished memories strengthened by this annual ritual but there was an added poignancy this year.

A whole decade had passed.

Two decades since the small band of gifted but under-challenged boys boarding at Greystones Grammar school had been labelled as 'bad'.

The label had stuck even as the four of them had blitzed their way to achieving the top four places in the graduation year of their medical schooling.

But now there were only three 'bad boys' and the link between them had been tempered by the fires of hell.

Minimally depleted bottles were lowered but the silence continued. A tribute as reverent as could be offered to anything that earned the respect of these men.

The sharp knock at the door was inexcusably intrusive and more than one of the men muttered a low oath. They ignored the interruption but it came again, more urgently this time, and it was accompanied by a voice.

A female voice. A frightened one.

'Sarah? Are you home? Oh, God…you *have* to be home. Open the door… *Please…*'

The men looked at each other. One shook his head in disbelief. One gave a resigned nod. The third—Max—moved to open the door.

Please, please…please…

Ellie squeezed her eyes tightly closed to hold back tears as she prayed silently, raising her hand to knock for the third time. What in God's name was she going to do if Sarah *wasn't* home?

It was enough to make her want to hammer on the door with both fists. Her arm moved with the weight of desperation only to find an empty space. Too late, Ellie realised the door was moving. Swinging open. It was all too easy to lose her balance these days and she found herself stumbling forward.

Staring at a black T-shirt under an unzipped, black leather biker's jacket. An image flashed into her head. She'd passed a row of huge, powerful motorbikes parked outside this apartment block and she hadn't thought anything of it.

Oh…God! She'd come to the wrong door and

here she was, falling into a bikers' den. A gang headquarters, maybe. A methamphetamine lab, even. Huge, powerful male hands were gripping her upper arms right now. Pulling her upright. Pulling her deeper into this dangerous den. Her heart skipped a beat and then gave a painful thump.

'Let me go,' she growled. 'Get your hands *off* me.'

'No worries.' The sexy rumble from somewhere well above her head sounded…what…tired? *Amused?* 'I'd just prefer you didn't land flat on your face on my floor.'

It was a surprisingly polite thing for a gang member to say. Ellie could do polite, too.

'I've made a mistake.' She had to step forward again to get her balance. It helped to drop the small bag she'd been carrying to plant both her hands on the chest in front of her and push. Good grief, it felt like a brick wall. Ellie risked an upward glance, to find the owner of the chest looking down at her. Dark hair. Dark eyes that held a somewhat surprised expression. No tattoos, though. No obvious piercings. And didn't he look a bit too *clean* to be part of a bikie gang?

She swung her head sideways and emitted a small squeak of dismay. There were two more of them. Staring at her. No, one was glaring. They were clad from head to toe in black leather. Jackets that were padded at the shoulders and elbows and tight pants that also had protective padding. Heavy boots. The gleam of zips and buckles might as well have been chains and knuckle-dusters. They were holding beer bottles. She had interrupted something and they weren't happy. There didn't seem to be quite enough air in this small room because there were three very large and potentially very dangerous men using it all up.

Ellie straightened to her full height, which was unfortunately only five feet three inches.

'I'm so sorry,' she said, as briskly as she could manage. 'I've come to the wrong door. I'm looking for Sarah Prescott. I'll…I'll be going now.'

She turned back to the door only to find the first man blocking her escape route simply by standing there and filling the space. Ellie swallowed. Hard.

'Look, I'm really sorry to have disturbed you.' She inched sideways. Maybe she could squeeze past and get to the door. She might have to leave her bag behind but that didn't matter.

The man didn't appear to move but somehow the door was swinging shut behind him.

'I…have to go,' Ellie informed him. Dammit, she could hear the fear in the way her voice wobbled.

'To find Sarah?'

'Yes.'

'Is it urgent?'

'Oh…*yes*.' Ellie had no trouble making this assertion. She even nodded her head vigorously for emphasis.

'Why?'

Ellie's jaw dropped. As if she'd start telling a complete stranger about any of this. If she had the time, which she didn't, why did he want to know anyway?

Lost for words, she stared up at this man.

'It's OK,' he said quietly. 'You're safe here.'

How did he know that those were the words she needed to hear more than anything? How did *she* know with such conviction that she could believe him?

For another heartbeat Ellie simply kept staring.

And then she burst into tears.

The heavy, straight fringe of deep chestnut hair made her face seem fragile as Max stared down at it. He saw this woman's fear and he saw the effect his words of reassurance had.

She let go.

She didn't even know him but she trusted that she was safe. Now he could feel the weight of responsibility pressing down on him. What had he been thinking?

And then those huge, hazel eyes filled with

tears and he groaned inwardly. This was the last straw.

No. As he put his arms around this small, unwanted visitor and felt the firm bulge of her abdomen, which had been disguised by her baggy sweater, his heart sank even further.

Somehow, in the space of just a heartbeat or two, he'd offered protection to a woman who looked as though she was running from something. Or someone.

A very pregnant woman.

'Max…' The word was a warning. 'What are you doing, man? She's come to the wrong apartment, that's all.'

'No.' Max held onto the body shaking with silent sobs and did his best to guide her towards the sofa. 'Sarah Prescott was the previous tenant here. She took off to the States last week.'

'What?' Max felt a determined push against his chest that felt familiar. *'No.'*

Tears were scrubbed from her face and she gave a rather unladylike sniff. 'She's going on Friday.

Tomorrow. That's why I'm here. I'm going to go with her.'

'She did go on Friday. Last Friday.' Max sighed and let his gaze drop to the oversized sweater. 'You really think they would have let you on an international flight? When are you due?'

Her mouth dropped open and he could see the wheels turning in her head. She realised he'd felt the shape of her body when he'd taken hold of her. A flush of colour stained pale cheeks but she said nothing.

Resentment at the intrusion into a private moment was long gone. Max could sense the spark of curiosity from the others now, albeit reluctantly, particularly on Jet's part. But this was a damsel in distress. She needed help.

'Come and sit down,' Max suggested. 'What's your name?'

'Ellie,' she said, but didn't move any closer to the sofa. 'Ellie Peters.'

'I'm Max. That's Rick, who's putting his helmet on the table over there, and this is Jet.'

That surprised her.

'His real name is James,' Max added. 'But he's always had a thing for flying and his hair's really black, see?'

Ellie gave a slow nod as she flicked a cautious gaze towards the other men.

Rick was near the window now. 'His hair's only that colour 'cause he dyes it,' he said casually.

Jet's snort told Rick he would pay for that comment later but Ellie's lips twitched. Good. She was starting to relax. Maybe they could find out why it was she needed to find her absent friend so urgently, offer some advice to solve the problem and send her on her way. The others had to head away themselves very soon and they didn't get together often enough to make sharing the last of this time a welcome prospect. No wonder Jet was looking so impatient.

'Can I get you a drink?' Max offered Ellie. His gaze dropped automatically to the bulge of her sweater. So obvious now he'd felt it. Curiously, he could still feel it. As part of that body shaking with sobs she'd tried so hard to stifle. A shape that seemed to be imprinted on his own body. She was eyeing the beer bottles on the table. 'I mean…water or something?'

'Hate to break up the party,' Rick drawled, 'but there's a guy on the street out here who seems rather interested in this apartment.'

Ellie's indrawn breath was a gasp. She slid sideways, making sure she wasn't in view. Closer to the wall now, she kept moving and peeped around the edge of the window frame.

'Oh…*no*…' The word was a groan. 'It's Marcus. I thought I'd lost him at the airport.'

'And who is Marcus?' Max stepped swiftly to look out of the window but the street below was deserted apart from a taxi and its driver.

'He's…um… He was my…' Ellie seemed to be finding it difficult to find the description she wanted. 'I was in a relationship with him. Briefly. It's been…hard to get away.'

The underlying message was unmistakable.

Max tried to curb the slash of anger. 'He's *stalking* you?'

'Ah…kind of, I guess.'

'Where have you come from?'

'Today? Wellington. I think he must have hired a private investigator who picked up on my air-ticket purchase. He must have flown down from Auckland to be at the airport by the time I arrived.'

'Auckland…of course…' Rick snapped his fingers. 'Thought the little weasel looked vaguely familiar.'

Everybody's head swung in Rick's direction. Max and Ellie spoke together.

'You *know* him?'

'Marcus Jones. Orthopaedic surgeon, yes?'

'Y-yes,' Ellie stammered, looking bewildered.

Rick addressed the others. 'Had a little run-in with him when I was working in Auckland Central a few years back.' The huff of expelled breath was not complimentary. 'Guy with a nasty spinal tumour. I was keen to try a new approach.

Risky but perfectly doable. Would have left him neurologically intact.'

The nod from Max and Jet accepted that Rick's judgement would have been correct.

'The weasel is persuasive. He talked the patient and his family into going with the standard protocol. Poor guy ended up quadriplegic and on a home ventilator. Probably dead by now.'

Max caught Jet's raised eyebrow and nodded. 'He follows the rules.'

'Hell, he thinks he can *make* the rules,' Rick said.

'Does he, now?' Max injected enough of an ominous tone into his query to earn approving glances from the other men. A glance at Ellie's wide eyes revealed that she had no clue what the unspoken conversation going on here was about but it certainly wasn't making her feel any more secure.

Should he take the time to tell her that one of the things that welded the three of them together was the shared conviction that sometimes some of the rules had to be broken? That they were all people who had no hesitation in doing exactly that if they considered it to be necessary?

He didn't have the time. The rap on his door was far more demanding than Ellie's knock had been.

'Open the door.' The owner of the voice was used to being in control. 'I know you're in there, Eleanor.'

Jet went to open the door.

'*No*,' Ellie breathed. 'Please…'

Max and Rick moved to stand on either side of Ellie.

Max tilted his head. 'He doesn't sound like he's going to go away without a little encouragement. You're safe here, remember?'

'Mmm.' The sound was hesitant but hopeful. It tugged at something deep inside Max.

'You'd like him to go away, wouldn't you?'

'Yes.'

'For good?'

'Oh…*yes*.'

Jet flung the door open.

'About time.' The small man in a pinstriped suit stepped into the apartment. 'Come on, Eleanor. I've got a taxi waiting for us.'

Ellie said nothing. Max could see the way her lips trembled even though she had them pressed tightly together.

The newcomer took another step further inside and it was then that he seemed to notice Ellie's companions. He looked over his shoulder at Jet, who had closed the door and was leaning against it, his arms folded and a menacing look on his face. Max almost grinned. No one could do menacing quite as well as Jet.

Rick earned a look then. And finally Max. Good thing they were all still in their leathers, having only just finished their annual road trip, which was part of their tribute to Matt. Even better that they were all at least six inches taller, considerably heavier and quite a lot younger than the dapper surgeon.

Marcus Jones cleared his throat. 'Who are these people, Eleanor?'

Ellie remained silent. She looked remarkably like a small, wild animal caught in the glare of oncoming headlights, Max decided before flicking his gaze back to the most recent arrival.

He watched the way Marcus swallowed, revealing his discomfort. This man was a bully, he realised. The thought that he'd had the opportunity to bully the woman standing beside him was more than enough to fuel his simmering anger.

The surgeon spread his hands in a contrived gesture of appeal and directed his words to the men in the room. 'Look, I don't know what she's told you but this is nothing more than a minor misunderstanding. Eleanor's my fiancée. She's pregnant with my child and I've come to take her home.'

Max felt Ellie sway slightly beside him. He put his arm around her shoulders and she leaned into him. He glanced down and met her eyes. He saw a silent plea for protection that no red-blooded man could have resisted. Especially an angry one.

'Funny,' he heard himself say mildly, 'Ellie told me the baby is mine, and you know what?' He speared the stranger with his gaze. 'I believe her.'

The silence was stunned and no wonder. Max was more than a little stunned himself by what he'd just said.

The baby is mine?

They were words he'd never expected to utter in his life and they were having a rather odd effect. Creating a weird tingle of something that felt curiously…pleasant. Good, even. They made him feel taller. More powerful.

Rick made a sound that could have been strangled laughter but was effectively disguised as a cough. Unseen by Marcus, Jet shook his head in disbelief and didn't bother to hide his smirk.

Max drew himself up to his full six feet three inches and didn't break his stare by so much as a blink.

'Eleanor…' Marcus narrowed his eyes. 'Are you

going to *say* something or just stand there like some kind of stuffed toy?'

Jet opened the door. 'The lady doesn't want to talk to you,' he said politely. 'Why don't you play nice and get lost?'

'Don't tell me what to do,' Marcus snapped. 'I happen to be the top surgeon in the orthopaedic department of Auckland Central Hospital. I don't care what kind of gang you belong to. Get in my way and you'll regret it.'

'What are you going to do to us?' Rick said softly. 'Botch some surgery perhaps and leave us to suffer on a ventilator for the rest of our lives?'

'*What* did you say?' The stare Rick received now was intense enough to send a prickle down Max's spine. This man was dangerous. He tightened his hold on Ellie. 'Good God…I don't believe it. You're that upstart neurology registrar who thought he knew more than I did.'

'It was a few years ago,' Rick reminded him. 'I'm actually a neurosurgical consultant these days.'

'And I'm an emergency medicine consultant,' Max informed him. 'Your status isn't helping you much here, mate.'

'I'm on an ED locum run while I'm in town,' Jet murmured. 'But I'm usually a medic with the SAS. Your threats don't hold much water, either.'

Max heard Ellie's sharp intake of breath. Had she really thought they were gang members, too? She'd still trusted him, though, hadn't she?

He liked that.

Whatever was going through her head, she seemed to be feeling braver.

'Go away, Marcus,' she said. 'I told you a very long time ago that I never wanted to see you again.'

Marcus Jones was looking less and less sure of himself. He shifted his feet and glanced over his shoulder at the open door behind him.

'She's with me now,' Max added for good measure. 'My woman. My baby.' He smiled grimly. 'Now get the hell out of here and don't come back. *Ever.*'

They all watched from the window as Marcus Jones scrambled into the waiting taxi and left.

Rick chuckled. 'Nice one, Max.'

Jet shook his head yet again. 'Yeah…you certainly pulled a good rabbit out of the hat. Gotta love you and leave you, though, man. It's getting late.'

'Sure is.' Rick was reaching for his helmet. 'Gotta go, too, mate. We'll catch up soon.'

'But…' The ground was shifting under Max's feet. His mates were about to desert him and Ellie was still here. What the hell was he supposed to do now?

His friends knew perfectly well they were dropping him in it. They were enjoying it, for God's sake. Grinning broadly, even.

Max walked to the door with them, doing his best to think of some way he could beg them to stay without becoming the brunt of their mirth for years to come. They were having none of it. Rick thumped him on the arm.

'You'll think of something,' he said. 'Hey…your woman, remember? *Your* baby.'

He could hear the echo of their laughter even well after the door closed behind them.

CHAPTER TWO

THE throaty roar of powerful bikes faded but Ellie could still feel the reverberations.

Or was she still shaking from the face-to-face encounter with Marcus Jones?

Unbidden, her legs took her to one of the chairs around a table and she sank down onto it. Her worst fear had been realised. Marcus had found her. He knew she was pregnant and sounded absolutely confident that the baby was his.

But she had won. Not completely, of course. Her legs were probably still shaky because she knew he wouldn't give up this easily but she had won this round thanks to a most unlikely team of dark, leather-clad angels. They were, without doubt, the most impressive array of masculinity she'd ever been this close to and they had stood up for her.

Protected her.

Sent Marcus Jones scurrying away with his tail between his legs.

He wouldn't like that.

The tiny smile Ellie had been quite unaware of, as she had thought of her guardian angels in action, faded abruptly.

'You OK?' A chair scraped on the tiled area of the floor as Max took a seat at the other end of the table. He pushed a black, full-faced helmet to one side, where it clunked against the trio of beer bottles.

'I'm fine.' The sound had caught Ellie's attention. 'I'm sorry I interrupted your party.'

The corner of Max's mouth lifted. 'Hey, if it had been a party there'd be a damn sight more than three lager bottles left over and they'd be empty, what's more.' He rubbed at his face. 'No…this was…a toast, that's all. A token one at that thanks to the guys having to work tonight. It's a bit of an annual ritual, I guess.' His voice softened into a sadness that tugged at Ellie's heart. 'An anniversary.'

She had been watching his face as he spoke. Such serious lines… His eyes were dark brown—a match for wavy hair that looked like it had been squashed under that helmet for some time. The odd, wayward end of a curl was valiantly poking out here and there, giving him a rather charmingly dishevelled look that was enhanced by the faint shadowing of his jaw.

She watched his fingers as he rubbed the uncompromising line of that jaw. Funny, but she could almost feel the catch of stubble on her own fingers. Just a little rough. As though he usually shaved at least once a day but hadn't bothered on this particular occasion.

He had shadows under his eyes too and lines that looked emotional rather than age related. He couldn't be much older than her. No more than his mid-thirties. The echo of his tone lingered.

'Not a happy anniversary?' The query was tentative. It was none of her business, after all, but she owed this man something. Rather a lot, actually, and if he wanted to talk about whatever was on his mind, the least she could do was take the time to listen.

He was watching *her* now. Warily. Then his gaze slid sideways and he sighed.

'There used to be four of us,' he said simply. 'See?'

He was indicating a silver framed photograph that had pride of place on the bookshelf beneath the window. Four young men, probably in their early twenties, were lined up in front of four gleaming motorbikes. They all wore leathers and held a helmet under one arm and they were all grinning. The picture was resonant with the thrill of being alive and young and with the promise the future held. Ellie recognised Max and Rick and the one with the odd name—Jet. The fourth man was shorter than the others and had wildly curly hair. He looked younger. As though he was out with his big brothers.

'Matthew died ten years ago today.'

'Oh…' Ellie stole this opportunity to let her gaze rest on his face again. The bond between the three men when they'd decided to protect her had been unmistakable. He was capable of caring very deeply for others, this man. He still cared about a member of their group who had been dead for ten years. He was also capable of very deep loyalty.

Heavens, he'd been prepared to protect her—a complete stranger. No wonder her instincts had told her so convincingly that he could be trusted.

'I'm sorry,' she said softly.

Max looked up. 'Fate has the oddest little twists sometimes,' he said with an attempt at a smile that came out with an endearing crookedness. 'Matt died because there were people who were protocol police. A bit like your friend, Mr Jones.'

'He's *not* my friend,' Ellie whispered fiercely, but Max didn't seem to hear her. He had closed his eyes. He had the most astonishingly long, dark eyelashes.

'There were rules in place and they had to be followed.' He opened his eyes again but he was seeing a very different place from where he was sitting with Ellie on this quiet Sunday afternoon. 'Their egos wouldn't allow them to even consider they might be wrong. We were fresh out of medical school and what consultant would bend rules just because we had a hunch? Or let us juggle rosters so we could keep an eye on Matt? Even he said he was fine. It was just a headache. He'd sleep it off.'

Max paused to drag in a slow breath but Ellie stayed silent. She was happy to listen even though she knew this story wasn't going to have a happy ending.

'Didn't help that we were legends for the way we partied but by the time we came off duty, Matt was in a coma from a ruptured aneurysm. They kept him on life support only long enough for his family to think about organ donation.'

Max was eyeing the bottles again as though he wanted a slug of something. 'They didn't want us around,' he continued tonelessly. 'And why would they? Any hint of trouble Matt had been in for the past ten years had been associated with us. His sister, Rebecca, was convinced we could have saved him if we'd tried a bit harder. It was the worst time ever. Finally, we got our bikes and took to the road for a good, hard blast. We came back to learn that they'd turned off the machines and Matt was gone.

'Anyway,' He shook his head, letting the memories go. 'We figured that Matt had been pillion that day. Riding out in style. So we do it every year. Go for a blast on the open road and then finish off with a nice, cold beer.'

'And I interrupted you.' Ellie's tone was full of remorse but Max smiled.

'But don't you see? We got the chance to play the heavies with one of them. Egotistical rule followers. The kind we didn't know how to deal with way back then. Take my word for it, it was a bonus.'

Max's smile was doing something very odd to Ellie.

This was the first time she had seen both sides of his mouth curl evenly. There was warmth there, unsullied by anything sad or grim. A warmth she could feel curling inside her, melting that hard knot of tension that was starting to make her back ache intolerably.

The adrenaline overload of the last thirty minutes or so was draining away to leave her utterly exhausted but that was OK because there was energy to be found in that smile, too. It really was quite extraordinary. It was just a shame she was too tired to smile back.

'So, that's my story.' Max raised an eyebrow as his face settled back into rather more intent lines. 'What's yours, Ellie Peters?'

He knew her full name was Eleanor now but he was still calling her Ellie. She liked that. Did she want to tell him her story?

Oh…yes.

Would he think less of her when he heard it?

Quite likely.

Ellie didn't want Max to think less of her so she didn't say anything.

Max waited patiently as the seconds ticked

past but he didn't take his gaze off her face. Ellie shifted uncomfortably, the ache in her back getting worse. Her stomach felt odd, too. As if it was trying to decide whether there was enough in it to be worth ejecting. Fortunately, there probably wasn't. She couldn't actually remember the last time she'd had something to eat. Last night?

'Was he right?' Max asked evenly. 'Is the baby his?'

Ellie recognised the new sensation as disappointment. She had no choice other than to let Max think less of her. She owed him honesty, if nothing else.

'Yes.'

A whisper. A tiny word but, man, it hurt. If only it *didn't* have to be the truth. Ellie's eyes prickled with unshed tears but Max didn't seem to react at all.

'How did you meet him?'

'I…I was his theatre nurse. In Auckland. He didn't even know my name for the longest time but then he suddenly noticed me and he started being nicer to me in Theatre. Nicer to everybody, actually.'

An eyebrow as dark as those enviable eyelashes quirked. 'He wasn't usually nice, then? No, don't tell me, let me guess.' The padded elbows of the leather jacket were resting on the table and Max steepled his fingers as he spoke. 'Bit of a temper?' His thumbs and forefingers touched each other. 'Instruments getting hurled around when he wasn't happy?' Ellie watched his middle and ring fingers make contact. 'People getting verbally beaten up on occasion?'

Ellie's gaze flicked up from watching his fingers. 'How do you know?'

The steeple was gone, fingers curling into fists. 'I know the type. Go on, what happened after this miraculous personality transplant?'

'He...um...asked me out.'

'And you fell into his arms?' The words were just a little too bland and Ellie cringed.

'No,' she said hurriedly. 'I wasn't interested but...' She sighed. 'Marcus was very persistent and…and he can be quite charming, believe it or not.'

'Oh, I believe it,' Max said grimly. 'Control freaks are notoriously capable of charming the birds out of the trees if that's what it takes to get what they want.'

Ellie took a deep breath. She wanted to get this confession over and done with. 'I went out with him,' she said in a rush. 'But only twice.'

Max leaned back in his chair. The look on his face said it all and why should she be surprised? Two dates and she got knocked up? But then he frowned.

'He's not a man who likes to take no for an answer, is he?'

Ellie bit her lip. She really didn't want to talk about this. To anyone. She didn't even want to have to *think* about it again.

Maybe something of the shame, and fear, of that night was in her face. Max certainly saw enough to make him curse. Softly but, oh, so vehemently.

'The *bastard*. Dammit, I wish we hadn't let him go unscathed. If we'd had *any* idea…'

Ellie's head shake was determined. 'No. It would only have made things worse. He'd win in the end. *Somehow*. He always does.'

'Not this time.'

Good heavens, he made it sound like a promise but, sadly, it wasn't one that Ellie could afford to accept. Not for herself or the baby. Or for Max and his friends. They all had careers within the medical world. Damage could be done on all sorts of levels.

'I'm going to get well away,' she assured Max. 'Out of the country. I'll change my name and start again somewhere he'll never find us.'

'Uh-uh.' The negative sound had a ring of finality.

'What?'

'You can't let him win.'

'I can't fight. I tried. I even threatened him if he wouldn't leave me alone and guess what? I lost my job. He managed to make me look totally incompetent in Theatre and laid an official complaint. Nobody would listen to my side and I got shifted sideways to work in a geriatric ward and even that wasn't enough for him.'

Max said nothing but he was listening hard.

'He was always there. Ready to make things better if I co-operated. There were apologies and promises and threats. Flowers and phone calls and endless text messages that all looked completely innocent on their own. He'd be waiting for me when I finished a shift sometimes and I'd never know whether he'd choose 6 a.m. or midnight. My flatmate, Sarah, got freaked out so I left town. I got a job in Wellington. Sarah left a few weeks later. Said she was still freaked because Marcus kept turning up, wanting to know where I was, and she couldn't cope, not when she had Josh to think about.'

Max nodded. 'I met Josh. Nice kid.'

'Did you know he's Sarah's nephew, not her son?'

'She did tell me. Her sister died in some kind of accident a couple of years ago?'

'That's right. Sarah was the only family member who could take him. He's only nine so I didn't blame her for being so worried. She blamed me, though, for the hassles Marcus caused. So much that she didn't talk to me for months.'

'Why didn't you go to the police?'

'Who would have listened to some nurse bad-mouthing a well-respected consultant surgeon? I'd already had a taste of his influence on people when I tried to defend my job in Theatre. I had a grudge. I had no evidence of anything other than romantic gestures and texts from a man most people considered charming.'

'Did you know you were pregnant when you left?'

Ellie shook her head. 'It didn't even occur to me because I was taking a low-dose pill to control painful periods and it worked so well I often didn't get them at all. It was months before I twigged and by then it was way too late to do anything about it…even if I…' She trailed off with a sigh.

This was getting worse by the minute. He'd think she was weak in having gone out with Marcus in the first place. Stupid not to consider the possibility of pregnancy. Even more stupid not to go to the police and maybe he had a thing against terminations for any cause and she would have considered it very seriously, God help her, because...

'Not the kind of man you would have picked to be the father of your baby?' There was a wealth of understanding in Max's voice and Ellie's breath came out in a whoosh of relief.

'No.'

'Could be worse,' Max said thoughtfully. 'The guy's not *that* bad looking.'

Ellie's jaw sagged.

'And he's obviously got well above average intelligence.'

Was he trying to make a *joke* out of this? *Unbelievable.* Maybe her judgment of his character had been woefully misguided.

'Bit on the short side,' Max continued. His

gaze rested on Ellie. 'And you're hardly a giant but...' He nodded. 'Maybe it'll be a girl. Petite and pretty, just like her mum.'

He was smiling at her again. 'Hey, if you'd gone to a sperm bank he would have looked pretty good on paper, wouldn't he? I'll bet his undesirable attributes are all due to nurture, not nature.'

The sharp flash of dismay—anger, even—that he could be belittling the nightmare she'd been living with for so many months gave way to something very different. Something rather wonderful. Something that made it OK that she loved this baby she was carrying. She didn't have to feel ashamed. Or guilty. Or terrified of what the future might hold for her child.

He'd not only made her feel safe, this man. He'd given her...hope.

Ellie's smile wobbled. 'Thank you.'

'No worries.' Max looked away. Was he embarrassed by the gratitude he might be seeing? 'So, do you know if it's a girl?'

'No.'

'You weren't tempted to ask the ultrasound technician?'

'I haven't had a scan.'

Too late, Ellie realised what she'd let slip as Max blinked at her. 'Excuse me?'

'I haven't had a scan,' she repeated. Did he not understand? 'If I'd gone to an antenatal clinic my name would have been recorded. I knew Marcus was trying to find me and I couldn't take that risk.'

'But didn't the hospital in Wellington get your details when you got a new job there?'

'I didn't get a job in a hospital. I went into the private sector. I had a job as a carer for a tetraplegic guy. I kept it up until very recently when the lifting got too much and then I finally managed to contact Sarah and she said she was going to the States and it seemed like the perfect solution so I sorted my passport and—'

'Whoa!' Max held up a hand. 'Rewind. Are you saying you've had *no* antenatal care? Not even a scan?'

'I'm twenty-eight,' Ellie said defensively. 'Young and healthy. I've had no problems. I've taken my own blood pressure at regular intervals and I even had the opportunity to test my own urine for protein and so on because the man I was caring for had dipsticks provided. I've taken all the recommended vitamin supplements and been careful with my diet. I had all the information I needed in my textbooks and I'm a nurse, for heaven's sake. I can take care of myself. I would have got help if there'd been any indication it was needed. I'm not stupid.'

The way his eyebrows lifted suggested that Max was reserving judgement on that score. 'How many weeks are you?'

'Thirty-six weeks and two days.'

'What position is the baby in?'

'I…' That was something Ellie had done her best to ascertain but would have to admit she hadn't succeeded in finding out. A small bottom and a head were hard to distinguish by palpation.

'You don't know, do you?'

Ellie had to look away. She pressed her lips together and encouraged the small flare of resentment she could feel forming.

'Where were you planning to give birth given your aversion to registering as a patient in a hospital?'

'I can go to a hospital. Somewhere else. Under a different name.'

'And if you happen to succeed in lying about your due date and actually get onto an international flight, how's that going to work if you go into labour at thirty thousand feet? Hours away from the nearest airport?'

He was angry. With *her*.

And it was unbearable.

He'd made her feel safe and then he'd given her hope and now he was taking those precious moments back. Ellie had never felt this miserable in her entire life.

So utterly *alone*.

Max was appalled.

He'd protected Ellie and now that he knew what

he'd been protecting her *from*, he could only be grateful that fate had put him in the right place at the right time.

And now she was going to endanger both herself and her unborn baby with this insane plan to throw herself into a lifetime of hiding and deceit.

He couldn't see her face at the moment because she had dipped her head under the weight of his harsh tone. He could see the copper gleam of that thick mane of hair, however. And the tip of a small, upturned nose. What had he said about the baby? That it might be a girl—petite and pretty like its mother? He'd meant it, but he could have said more.

He could have suggested it might have that gorgeous colouring of her hair and eyes that would demand the attention of anybody. He might not be able to see her arms hidden beneath the wide sleeves of that sweater but he could guarantee the bone structure was as fine as her face and hands.

What he could see was the way they were wrapped around her lower body right now.

Fiercely protective. And he could see the slump of her shoulders as though she thought the entire world was against her.

Hadn't she been through enough without him getting on her case as well?

'Sorry,' he said sincerely. 'I don't want to make this any worse for you. I'd like to help, if I can.'

She looked up and caught his gaze and Max couldn't look away. He'd remembered the attractive colour of her eyes but he must have forgotten their impact. He could *feel* that gaze. Like a physical touch. A hand-hold, maybe. One that asked for comfort. Or strength. He could give her that much, couldn't he?

'You wouldn't have a forwarding address for Sarah, would you?'

'No.' Max frowned. 'You do know why she decided to take off for the States in such a hurry, don't you?'

'Not really. She didn't say much in her email. I got the impression she was making a new start. Wanting a new life?'

'No. That wasn't the reason.'

Ellie looked horrified. 'She was trying to get further away from *me*?'

'No. Did she not tell you about Josh? About him being diagnosed with leukaemia six months ago?'

'Oh, my God!' Ellie breathed. 'No. I knew she was worried about him when I left. She thought he was being affected by the stressful situation. It was one of the reasons I left Auckland.'

'He didn't get diagnosed until they came down here. He got a lot sicker fast and she decided she had to try and find his father so that the possibility of a bone-marrow transplant would be there. She finally managed to track down the man on his birth certificate and found out he's a doctor working in California. She decided the best way to deal with it was to take Josh to meet him. Too easy to just say no with an email or phone call. She's planning to stay long enough to have the transplant done in the States if it's possible.'

'She might need help looking after him. I could

do that. Poor Sarah. She needs a friend if nothing else.'

Her determination might be admirable but the wobble in Ellie's voice showed that she knew as well as he did that she was heading down a dead-end street with that plan.

'You can't go to the States right now, Ellie,' he said gently. 'Give it up.'

'Australia, then. That's only a few hours away.'

'Do you have any friends or relatives over there?'

'I know someone in Darwin.'

'That's nearly as far as the States. What about this side of Australia? Sydney or Melbourne or Brisbane?'

Ellie sighed. 'No.'

'How will you manage on your own?'

'I can get a job. I'm good at what I do.'

'I'm sure you are.' Max repressed a sigh. 'But do you think you'd get a position as a theatre nurse without having to produce a documented record of your qualifications? Without them wanting to know where you were last employed? Without talking to people there?'

Ellie looked away again. 'Yeah…I know.' Defeat darkened her words. 'I keep thinking and thinking about it and it's going round and round in my head and I just keep hoping I'll think of something that might work. Some way out.'

She gave him a quick glance and he could see that her eyes shimmered with tears. 'And I can't. I just have to take one day at a time and think about what I need to do *today*. For the next few hours, even.'

'What you need to do today is to make sure that everything's OK with you and your baby.'

Her nod was resigned. 'I'll go and see a doctor tomorrow, I promise. I'll find a midwife.'

'And you'll have the baby in a hospital?'

She shook her head. 'I *can't*. What if Marcus found out? What if he got the chance to do a DNA test or something and got evidence that it *is* his baby? He'd take it away from me.'

Ellie was gripping the table now. She pushed

herself to her feet. 'I'm *not* going to let that happen. Not to me and especially not to this baby. *My* baby.' She turned away with the obvious intention of leaving.

'Hey…my baby, too…kind of.' Max was on his feet. He had to stop her going. If she left, he'd have no way of helping her and he'd taken on a responsibility back then when he'd claimed paternity. OK, it had been pretence and he could give it up now but oddly it seemed to be getting stronger.

Ellie got halfway across the room as she made a direct line for her small overnight bag that still sat near the door. But then she stopped abruptly. She put her arms around herself again and then, to Max's horror, she doubled over with an agonised cry of pain. It was then that he saw the dark stain on the legs of her jeans.

Had her waters broken?

He was by her side in an instant. Holding her. Helping her to lie down, right where she was. He was touching her and when he took his hand away, he saw the unmistakable smears of blood on his fingers.

'Don't move, Ellie,' he said. 'It's going to be all right. I'm just going to call for an ambulance.'

CHAPTER THREE

THE wail of the ambulance siren still echoed in his head as Max followed the stretcher carrying Ellie into the emergency department of Dunedin's Queen Mary hospital.

The sound had been the consistent background to a blur of activity that he had orchestrated from the moment Ellie had collapsed on his floor. He had been the one to place the large-bore IV cannula to allow vital fluids to be administered to counteract the blood loss. He had inserted a second line when it had become apparent that her blood pressure was already alarmingly low and her level of consciousness was rapidly dropping. It was Max who kept an eye on the ECG monitor to see what effect the blood loss might have on her heart rhythm and increased the level of oxygen being given as the reading of circulating levels slowly deteriorated.

This was far worse than any complication he might have imagined her encountering on an international flight. She would have been in trouble if this had happened only hours ago on a short domestic hop. Or out on the street before she had knocked so unexpectedly on his door.

She was in trouble anyway.

So was the baby.

Not that he could afford to worry about the infant just yet. He knew that the mother's condition was the priority. He had dealt with such cases in his department more than once. Ruptured ectopic pregnancies. Uterine ruptures. Trauma. But this wasn't some unknown woman who'd been rushed into his department by an ambulance with its siren wailing urgently.

This was Ellie and he'd promised her she was safe now.

'Antepartum haemorrhage,' he told the startled-looking triage nurse as the stretcher burst through the electronic doors into a brightly lit department.

'Max! What on earth are you doing here?'

He ignored more than one head turning in his direction. Maybe this wasn't the way he usually arrived at work and he rarely turned up wearing his bike-riding leathers but it was no excuse for unprofessional behaviour from his colleagues.

'Is Trauma One free?'

'Yes. We got the radio message. Someone from O and G is on the way down.' The nurse followed the rapidly moving stretcher. So did the receptionist, who was clutching a clipboard.

'We haven't got a name,' the clerk said anxiously.

'Ellie,' Max snapped. They were through another set of double doors now, in the best-equipped area in the department to deal with a critical case. The paramedics stopped the stretcher right beside the bed with its clean, white sheet. Staff were waiting, having been primed to expect them, and they were wearing their aprons and gloves, ready to begin a resuscitation protocol. They all knew their first tasks. The portable monitoring equipment from the ambulance would have to be switched over to the built-in equivalents. A junior nurse held a pair of shears, ready to cut away Ellie's clothing. A trolley was positioned near the head of the bed, an airway roll already opened in case intubation was necessary.

It was no surprise to see who was ready to control both the airway of this patient and the running of this emergency scenario. Jet was wearing theatre scrubs now and had a stethoscope slung around his neck. There was nothing unprofessional about his immediate reaction to seeing who had come in with this patient. He didn't even blink.

'On my count,' he said smoothly. 'One, two… three.'

There was a pool of blood on the stretcher as they lifted Ellie across to the bed. She groaned and her eyes flickered open.

'It's OK,' Max said, leaning closer. 'We're in

the hospital now, Ellie. Jet's here and he's going to look after you. We're all going to look after you.'

Her eyes drifted shut again.

'GCS is dropping.' Max tried to sound clinical. Detached. It didn't work.

Jet was holding Ellie's head, making sure her airway was open. He was watching the rapid rise and fall of her chest and his gaze went to the monitor as the oxygen saturation probe on her finger began relaying the information he wanted.

He frowned and flicked the briefest glance at Max. 'What the hell happened?' he murmured.

'Massive haemorrhage. Seemed to come from nowhere as soon as she stood up. Severe abdominal pain as well.'

The clerk was still in the room, hovering behind the nursing staff who were changing ECG leads, hanging the bags of fluid and getting a blood-pressure cuff secured.

'What's Ellie's last name?' she asked. 'How old is she?'

A registrar had his hands on her swollen abdomen. 'It's rigid,' he announced. 'Is she in labour? What's the gestation?'

'Thirty-six weeks and two days,' Max said.

Ellie was almost naked now. Totally vulnerable. Exposed to an expanding team of medical personnel. Someone from the obstetric department had arrived, closely followed by a technician pushing a portable ultrasound machine. Jet was holding a mask over Ellie's face and frowning as he watched the numbers changing on the overhead monitor.

'Ellie...' He had his mouth right beside his ear and was speaking loudly. 'Can you hear me? Open your eyes.'

She wouldn't want to, Max thought. This would have to be absolutely terrifying.

'Are there any relatives who could give me her details?' the clerk persisted. 'Did her husband come in with her? Or...her partner?' The woman knew she was failing in her task but she made yet another effort. 'The father of the baby?'

That flicked a switch in Max's head and its effect was magnified by how vulnerable Ellie was. How much trouble she was in right now. He had tried to protect her and somehow he had stepped into a new nightmare and was still by her side. Was she aware of what was happening? Still terrified? Did she know he was here?

She had been so determined to stay away from hospitals to protect her child. Maybe the best thing he could do for her at this moment was to respect that determination and carry on with what had already worked once.

'Yes,' he said clearly. 'I'm the father.'

Somebody dropped something metallic on the far side of the room and the sound rang out in the suddenly still moment following his statement. Jet uttered a low profanity but his gaze was still fixed on the monitor and the sound could well have been taken to be concern at a new development in Ellie's condition. Max was close enough to speak to his friend without being overheard by anyone else.

'I'll explain later,' he murmured. 'Just back me up.'

The clerk was happy, scribbling on the sheet of paper attached to the clipboard. 'Surname?' she chirped briskly.

Oh, Lord. If she got registered under her real name, they have to deal with Marcus Jones turning up and he'd have plenty of time to get here. Even if things went better than any of them could expect in this room, there was no way Ellie would be getting discharged in a hurry.

There was no time to think. In for a penny, in for a pound.

'McAdam,' he said wearily. 'We're married.'

The nurse, who was sticking on the leads required for a twelve-lead ECG, looked up, open-mouthed, and others exchanged astonished glances but the clerk knew she was on a roll.

'How old is your wife?'

'Twenty-eight.'

'Date of birth?'

As if *he'd* know. This had gone far enough. Far too far, judging by the look Jet slanted his way.

'Leave it,' Max growled. 'We can sort the paperwork later.'

'But we need—'

'Get out,' Jet snapped. 'We're busy.' He looked up, avoiding Max but catching most others in the room as he issued his orders.

'I'm going to intubate,' he warned. 'Oxygen saturation levels have fallen far enough. We need a central venous line in. And an arterial line.'

'I'll do that,' Max offered.

Jet gave his head a negative jerk. 'On your wife? I don't think so.' He nodded at his registrars, giving them the signal to get started. 'Get some bloods off as well. We need to know her blood group. Stat.'

'I'd like a rhesus factor and antibodies, too.' The obstetric consultant was watching the technician begin the ultrasound examination. 'Looks like we've got a central placenta praevia here and she's in labour. Fully dilated.'

* * *

Less than an hour later, in the middle of the life-and-death battle to save Ellie Peters, she gave birth to a tiny baby girl.

There was a paediatric team amongst the crowd in Trauma One now. And a consultant from the intensive care unit, who was a specialist in dealing with haemorrhagic shock resulting from such massive blood loss. Ellie was being cared for. The baby was being carefully assessed.

Having been forced onto the sidelines due to his own admission of involvement, there seemed to be nothing for Max to do other than watch. He was torn between watching the monitors to evaluate the success of the treatment Ellie was receiving and staring at the scrap of humanity the paediatric consultant was bent over.

'She's small but doing OK,' she pronounced eventually. 'I'm happy with her breathing but the heart rate's a bit on the slow side. Did I hear someone say the father is here?'

Ellie was deeply unconscious. The obstetrician

was happy that the bleeding had ceased now that delivery was complete but the control of the blood loss might have come too late. The mother of this tiny baby was now on a ventilator to manage what looked like adult respiratory distress from fluid loss. Jet and the ICU consultant were worried about her kidneys. Her production of urine had virtually ceased and her most recent blood test showed deterioration in renal function.

Max had done what he'd thought was the right thing in continuing the pretence that he was the baby's father and he couldn't back out now. Jet wouldn't say anything because he'd asked him to back him up and the brotherhood that they made up, along with Rick, was glued together with a loyalty that would never be broken. There were plenty of other people ready to say something, however. To point him out and draw him into the case that this department would be talking about for a very long time.

'You're the father?' The paediatrician didn't know him so there was no undertone of astonishment. 'Good. Come with us. We're going to take your daughter upstairs and she'll need you.'

Max took a step towards the group looking after the baby. And then another. And then he stopped.

'I can't…' He looked over his shoulder at Ellie. And then back to the baby, now dried and wrapped in soft, warm towels. What the hell had he got himself into here?

Jet's voice was calm. 'Nothing you can do for Ellie at the moment, mate,' he said. 'We're going to transfer her up to ICU very soon. Best you go with the baby. I'll come and update you as soon as I can.'

And wherever the baby was being taken, whether it was a maternity ward or the paediatric ICU, it would be a more private place, Jet's tone suggested. They would be able to talk about this. Hopefully, they might even be able to sort out the mess Max had created.

It seemed a reasonable plan. Max wasn't due on duty here in the emergency department until first thing tomorrow morning. They had a whole night to sort things out. Stepping back from taking any responsibility for Ellie might be a good first step. He took another step towards the baby and nodded.

'Let's go,' he agreed.

'How would you feel about holding her?'

'Ah…I'm not sure that's a great idea right now, is it?'

The paediatrician also took another glance at the monitor where the newborn baby's heart rate was slowing down yet again.

'It could help. Have you heard of kangaroo care?'

'No.' Max was staring at the baby in the plastic crib. It was lying on its side, a soft white hat covering the dark whorls of hair on its head. One arm was bent, a tiny starfish hand resting on its cheek.

Max hadn't spent this long in the company of a baby this small…ever. He'd participated in a fair few deliveries, of course, throughout his training and then in a short run on O and G but it was a rare occurrence in Emergency and the babies were always whisked off to places like this paediatric intensive care unit. He'd never had a reason to stay involved. He didn't now, except as a fraud.

He shouldn't really be here at all.

'It's been around since the late seventies,' the paediatric consultant broke into his guilt. 'But it's gaining quite a following. It's basically skin-to-skin contact with a parent. As long as the infant is medically stable, there's no reason not to use it and it's been shown to improve oxygenation and respiratory rates. It can actually make a significant difference to something like bradycardia.'

'Skin-to-skin?' Max couldn't keep the dismay out of his voice. 'Are you kidding me?'

'You don't sit around naked.' The doctor smiled. 'In fact, the baby needs to be under your own clothing to help maintain body temperature stability.' Her smile became reassuring rather than amused. 'I know she looks tiny and fragile and that her arrival was a bit unexpected...'

'You have no idea,' Max murmured.

'And I know you're worried about Ellie,' she continued, 'but this is a way to help everybody, including—maybe especially—yourself.'

'Oh?' Max was listening now. He needed to help himself. Fast. 'How, exactly?'

'You'll be doing what Ellie can't do at the moment, which is caring for her baby. You could well make a big difference medically for this little one.' She was watching him and a tiny frown line appeared. 'If you're really not comfortable, then I can get one of the nursing staff to do it, but it's far better if it's a parent. It can be a way of bonding that could make all the difference to the stress of the next few days.'

Max had the sensation of being trapped in a kind of glass box. He was being watched. By the paediatrician and her registrar. By the nurse who was hovering near the crib. Even by other nurses in this unit as they went about their own tasks. They all seemed to have paused right now to hold their breath and see what he was going to do.

They all believed that he was this baby's father and what kind of a father wouldn't want to do something that might help his kid? If it became obvious that he had no need—or, let's face it, desire—to bond with this infant, people might start asking questions. Gossiping at the very least, and the less any of this was talked about the better. For Ellie's sake.

Which was how all this had started, wasn't it?

He really would have to be more careful next time, he decided with a wry inward smile as he found himself nodding and then being guided to the comfortable armchair rolled into this corner of the PICU.

A nurse took the layers away from the baby. They left her with a nappy and her hat on, an oxygen saturation monitor clipped to a minuscule toe and some unobtrusive sticky dots and soft wires that connected her to a cardiac monitor. She was mostly naked, Max noted with some alarm. Small and pink and awkward-looking, with stick-like arms and legs.

'Keep her prone and upright,' the paediatrician advised. 'The nurses will keep an eye on you both and levels are set for an alarm to go off if the oxygen levels or cardiac rhythm need interventions.'

Max had sacrificed the neck of his T-shirt so that he didn't need to discard any of his own clothing. The vertical cut allowed him to fold the neckline down so that the baby's face would be uncovered. He heard the whimper of the baby as she was picked up.

Good grief…he really didn't want to do this. Was it too late to back out?

An alarm began to sound. A slow bell that pinged ominously. Maybe the baby didn't like the idea, either. Her heart rhythm was jumping erratically.

'Does she need to go back in the crib?' Max tried not to sound too hopeful.

'Let's see how we go for a minute or two.'

With an inward sigh, Max held up the bottom of his old, soft T-shirt while a nurse positioned the baby and then covered her. A layer of the leather jacket came next and then she helped him put his arm in the right place for support. He felt awkward. Uncomfortable.

He could feel the baby wriggle against his chest, moving tiny limbs as if in protest. He could feel the miniature chest heaving as she attempted to breathe and cry at the same time but the effort seemed exhausting and the movements diminished.

Max took a cautious glance downwards and found the baby's eyes were open. So dark they looked black and they were fixed on him. He took a deep, careful breath and let it out very slowly.

'Look at that.' The paediatrician sounded delighted. 'Heart rate's coming up and it's steady.'

They waited another minute as Max sat as still as humanly possible.

'Looking good,' came the expert verdict. 'We'll leave you to it, Max.'

'Ah…' He watched as staff began to disperse. To stop watching, even, from all over the unit.

Any second now and he would be virtually on his own. 'How long should I stay here?'

'The longer the better,' a nurse said cheerfully. 'As long as you can, anyway.'

Max tipped his head back and closed his eyes. He breathed. In and out. He could feel the baby breathing. In that first long, quiet minute of being left to himself he could even feel the baby's heart beating. A soft, rapid ticking against his chest. Almost on top of his own heart.

Weird.

He opened his eyes and tilted his chin so he could look down again.

The baby was still awake. Still watching him with a curiously intent gaze that managed to look utterly bewildered at the same time.

'Mmm,' Max murmured sympathetically. 'I know just how you feel. But don't worry. We'll get it all sorted out in no time.'

'Whoa! What are you *doing*?'

'Oh, *man...*'

Rick, closely followed by Jet, had come into a now dimly lit PICU to find Max still in the armchair, with a tiny baby nestled on his chest beneath his leather jacket.

'Shh…don't wake her up.'

Rick's eyebrows were sky high. 'I bumped into Jet as he was coming out of the big people ICU,' he said in a stage whisper. 'Thought I'd come and say hi and…' His grin widened. 'I'm sure glad I did. Wouldn't have missed *this* for quids. What *are* you doing?'

'Being a kangaroo,' Max muttered. 'Go away.'

Jet was looking at the monitors. 'Kid looks stable enough,' he said. 'Why don't you put it back to bed and we'll go get a coffee or something.'

Max sighed. 'Because every time I try and put her down she goes into a bradycardia and the oxygen levels drop.'

The nursing staff hadn't missed the arrival of Max's friends. More than one of them was finding a task that necessitated getting a lot closer to this extraordinary scene. Three large men and one very small baby.

'She loves her daddy,' the closest one said with a smile directed at Rick.

He smiled back. 'And who wouldn't?'

The nurse giggled. Max could swear she even batted her eyelashes at Rick. He sighed again.

'What's the story, Jet? How's Ellie doing?'

'On dialysis,' Jet said grimly. 'Renal function hasn't picked up yet and there's still some concern about her lungs. They're going to keep her sedated and on the ventilator, at least overnight.'

'Prognosis?'

Jet shrugged. 'She's hanging in there. Could go either way.'

Max swallowed. What was going to happen to this baby if Ellie didn't make it? He should be worried that he'd put his hand up as her only available relative but, instead, he found himself more worried about what life might have in store for this tiny girl.

Rick was leaning closer. 'Kinda cute, isn't it?'

He was grinning again. 'You know, I think I can see the family likeness.'

Jet snorted. He took a glance over his shoulder as if his scowl might be enough to ensure that the staff minded their own business for a while.

'How long are you going to keep this up, Max?'

Max said nothing. He was quite used to the feel of the baby against him now. In fact, at some point during the last couple of hours he'd experienced an odd sense of relief when the contact was re-established and things had settled down again. He wasn't going to make another attempt to put the baby back in her plastic crib any time soon. Maybe it wouldn't feel right until he knew whether or not her mother was going to survive.

Rick's smile had finally faded. 'Jet told me what happened in ED.' His mouth quirked again briefly. 'And if he hadn't told me, I would have found out pretty damn quick. The whole hospital is buzzing with the news of your sudden fatherhood, mate.'

'I'll bet.'

'I mean, it was one thing to tell the weasel you were the father so that he'd go away but...' Rick sucked in a long breath, an eloquent sound that encompassed the depth of the trouble Max had got himself into here.

'The guy raped her,' Max said quietly.

There was a moment's silence. Max could feel an echo of his own reaction to that information. The way it changed things. The anger on Ellie's behalf. On behalf of all women, really. They all liked women. A lot. He could sense the way his friends stilled. He saw Jet's hands curl into fists.

'And then he got her fired,' he added. 'When she tried to get away from him. He's been stalking her ever since.' He cleared his throat. 'And I told her she was safe.'

Another moment of silence as Rick and Jet absorbed and then accepted the implications.

'She won't be safe until she's well enough to look after this baby and get away.'

'She'll never be safe.' Rick's eyes were narrowed. 'The *bastard*.'

'Anyway...' Max didn't want to consider the future right now. The present was more than enough to deal with. Especially given that the baby was stirring. Woken by the intense conversation around it, perhaps. Or maybe it could sense the tension in the body it rested against.

The whimper became a warbling cry that made both Rick and Jet shift their feet uncomfortably. It also brought a nurse, who was carrying a bottle.

'Looks like it's dinnertime,' she said. 'Here you go, Daddy.' She handed Max the bottle.

'Maybe you better do this,' he muttered.

The baby's cry strengthened. Jet's pager sounded and he reached for it to read the message with obvious relief as Max fumbled with the bottle, trying to fit the teat into the tiny mouth.

'Gotta go,' Jet said. 'Sorry, mate. I'll get back later.'

'I'll come with you,' Rick said. Clearly this experience was rapidly losing its entertainment value.

Jet slanted a backward glance at Max. 'You

want me to arrange cover for your ED shift tomorrow?'

The baby's mouth had finally closed over the teat and she was trying to suck. Max tilted the bottle to help. The baby sucked harder, her dark gaze fixed on the man who didn't seem to know what he was doing. But then she tasted the milk and the sucking settled into a rhythm.

'Max?' Jet prompted.

'Yeah…cover would be good.' Max couldn't break the eye contact with the infant so he didn't even try and look up. 'I'm not going anywhere for a while.'

CHAPTER FOUR

SHE was lost.

It was dark. *So* dark. And maybe she was in a forest. There was danger. Animals or tree branches that scratched and bit. Things to trip over so that she landed hard enough to hurt herself because there was pain that wouldn't go away.

And fear.

She was running but so confused she couldn't tell whether she was running away from something that terrified her or towards something that she wanted so badly it was worth going through this terrible journey.

Weirdly, in spite of the pain and the fear, she felt protected. As though something…no, some*one*… was watching over her. A guardian angel but one so dark it was invisible. She thought she could detect a ripple in the inky shadows at times but then it would vanish, often under the onslaught of new pain, and then she would be in the dark again. Utterly forlorn.

Time was irrelevant. She had been in this place for ever so when it changed and light began to filter in, the new development was even more confusing. Scary.

'Ellie? Can you hear me?'

Yes…but she had no idea who this voice belonged to. She'd heard it before, she knew that much. And she liked it. She liked it very much because it made her feel…safe.

Talk some more, she begged silently. I want to feel your voice.

No…shouldn't that be hear? Except she *could* feel it. It wrapped around her like the softest blanket to keep her warm and yet it had a rough edge that rumbled its way through her ears and brain and into every part of her body. Through places that hurt and somehow it softened the pain so that it became no more than a background ache. Unimportant. The voice went right into her bones.

'Can you open your eyes?' it asked.

Ellie tried but they felt glued shut. Her eyelids were made of something so heavy it was impossible for tiny muscles to lift them. She could feel something, though. An encouraging kind of flutter.

'Wake up, Ellie.' The voice was also encouraging. 'There's someone here who would love to meet you properly.'

She tried again. Tried really hard because the owner of the voice wanted her to and that made it important to succeed. So important that nothing else mattered for the moment and even the ache deep within was forgotten. And slowly she achieved her goal. Her eyes were open and it was bright. Too bright. Her eyes stung and all she could see was a blur.

A very large, dark blur that reminded her fleetingly of the nasty place she'd been in for ever. The flash of memory was disturbing but the remnant of fear was gone just as quickly, leaving something oddly pleasant in its wake. This blur was like the shadow of that guardian angel. The one she'd tried so hard to catch sight of properly but which had always been just out of reach. Evaporating into the darkness.

The dreamlike wisp evaporated as well as Ellie blinked, adjusting to the light and letting the face swimming above hers come into focus.

Dark hair. Waves that were almost curls with small ends here and there that refused to behave and created a roguish frame for a face that had very definite lines and a jaw that was dark and rough and hadn't seen a razor for several days.

Dark eyes that were watching her very intently and a mouth that was tilting into a soft smile. The most beautiful smile Ellie had ever seen in her life.

'Hi, there,' the voice said. 'How're you doing?'

Ellie's lips felt stiff, as though they hadn't been used in quite a while. She tried to say something but her throat hurt and the only sound that emerged was a rusty squeak. She swallowed carefully and blinked again. Cautiously but very quickly in the end, just in case this was a dream and the man with the beautiful smile would vanish if she closed her eyelids for too long.

Her head was swirling with incomplete images and thoughts. She knew she was in a bed. In a hospital because she knew that familiar smell so well and there were equally recognisable sounds like the soft beeping of pagers and monitoring equipment. She could see the sharp edges of that equipment in her peripheral vision and she could hear echoes of voices that had long since stopped speaking. Urgent voices. Saying things like '*massive haemorrhage*' and '*Trauma One*' and '*blood group and cross-match. Stat*'.

Paralysed by the kaleidoscope happening inside her head, Ellie focused on those intent dark eyes above her.

'You're in the intensive care unit,' the voice said calmly. 'You've been pretty sick for a couple of days but you're going to be all right. You're off the ventilator now and your lungs are doing well. So are your kidneys. How's your throat? It's probably a bit sore after having a tube in it for so long.'

There was a frown in those eyes now. He was worried about something. *Her?* That was nice. Ellie liked that she was important enough for him to be worried about her. Maybe he'd smile at her again.

'I'm Max—remember? You came to the apartment to find Sarah but she wasn't there. And then you got into trouble. You went into labour and—'

Ellie could feel her eyes widening. Her skin was prickling as though the blanket the voice had provided was being stripped off, leaving her exposed to the elements. The sense of safety was gone, too. She could feel the fear of that awful forest place crowding around her. Something was happening in her brain. An almost painful series of jolts as pieces fell into place.

Sarah. Marcus. Her *baby…*

'She's fine,' Max said softly. 'See?'

His head tilted and Ellie's gaze followed the downward trajectory of his. Down his body to where his arms were cradling something. She couldn't see what it was until Max tipped forward and there, nestled in blankets, was a tiny face. A sleeping, newborn baby.

'*Oh…*' The sound forced its way past her sore, dry throat. 'Is that…?'

She knew it was. She could *feel* it but she needed to be told as well. To make sure she wasn't dreaming.

'Sure is,' Max said. 'This is your daughter, Ellie. Would you like to hold her?'

Ellie nodded. She couldn't say anything because her already tight throat was now entirely choked by tears. She could feel them rolling down her face as Max carefully placed the baby on her chest and then helped her move her arms to cradle the infant. He pushed IV tubing attached to her arm to one side and then he looked up, past Ellie.

'Could you grab an extra pillow or two?' he asked someone. 'Let's try and prop Ellie up a bit more.'

Her arms felt so weak Ellie was frightened

she'd let go but Max seemed to understand because he kept his hands on top, supporting her. A nurse came and tucked another pillow beneath her shoulders and an extra one under her head. A rush of dizziness faded and Ellie found she could blink her tears away and actually see her baby properly for the first time.

Her eyes were still closed, a fan of dark lashes sitting on each cheek like butterflies. A tiny button of a nose and a mouth pursed into a perfect cupid's bow.

'Isn't she beautiful?'

There was a note of wonder in his voice and something more. Something that was enough to make Ellie lift her gaze for an instant but Max was intent on the tiny face in her arms and he didn't look up so she couldn't get any clue to that confusing undertone.

She didn't have the energy to try and understand. Didn't even have the inclination to try because there was something far more important to think about. Something so wonderful that really it was no surprise that Max seemed to share what she couldn't begin to put into words.

This was her baby.

Her daughter. It was a *girl* and she was—

'Is she—?' Ellie's voice caught. Suddenly, she was too scared to ask.

'She's perfect.' Max sounded…good grief… *proud*? 'Ten little fingers, ten little toes. She's feeding well. Fifty grams up on two days ago.'

'What...?' Again, this was disturbing enough to make her stop feasting her eyes on the perfect features of her baby. 'My God…how long…?'

'Have you been in here?' Max looked up this time and there was sympathy in his eyes as he completed her horrified question. 'Three days, Ellie. This little button was born at seven minutes past six on Sunday.'

It was too much to take in. Ellie could have accepted feeling like this if she'd been coming round from, say, a general anaesthetic for an emergency Caesarean but her precious baby had been in the world for three whole days without her mother's knowledge, let alone her care and protection.

Panic was edging closer and Ellie found she was struggling to take a breath. She had to take in enough air to warn Max. To demand that they let her out of this bed so that she could be with her baby and take care of her. Or at least for them to bring the baby in here so that she could watch over her. Every second of every hour.

'*Ellie.*'

The tone was firm enough for her to realise this wasn't the first time he'd said her name. '*Listen* to me.'

The words were a command but were delivered in what was virtually a whisper. What Max was about to say was imperative.

And private.

Gulping like a stranded fish, Ellie blinked frightened tears into submission and fixed her gaze on Max. He took a quick look around them and then back at her.

'Remember how I told Marcus I was the baby's father and it made him go away?'

Ellie managed a nod.

'Well, I told them that here too and everyone believes it.'

That's what it had been, Ellie realised. That odd note in his voice. The way he'd been holding this tiny baby. He had looked and sounded for all the world like a besotted new father.

So he had been acting? To protect them?

Ellie blinked again, this time in bewilderment. He was either an incredibly good actor or her brain wasn't functioning at anywhere near normal levels of acuity. No, it had to be acting if everyone else believed it as well.

'There's more.' Max leaned closer. He could have been admiring the baby and he even used the tip of his middle finger to stroke the infant's cheek gently but his intention seemed to have been to put his mouth close enough to Ellie's ear to ensure that no one overheard.

'I didn't give them your real name,' he told her.

'And…um…I wasn't thinking too straight at the time so I told them…'

He sounded almost embarrassed, Ellie thought. What kind of weird name had he come up with?

'I told them that your surname was McAdam.'

Nothing wrong with that, Ellie decided with relief. It was a perfectly nice name.

'OK,' she whispered.

There was a moment's silence. Ellie could feel how still Max was. So still she was only aware of the tiny movements in her arms as her baby breathed and stirred slightly in slumber. She was used to the feel of those tiny limbs moving. It was like she'd lost part of herself but had found it again only now the movements were on the outside, instead of safely enclosed in her womb.

Max was still quiet. He seemed to be waiting for something. A breath audible enough to be a sigh escaped his lips.

'That's *my* name, Ellie.'

'Oh…' Well, that was OK, too. She didn't mind borrowing his name for a little while. As long as he didn't mind. But maybe he did. The continued silence was starting to feel uncomfortable.

'I…ah…told them we were married,' Max said, so softly Ellie was sure she hadn't heard correctly.

She could remember what had happened at the apartment. That he'd claimed he was the baby's father and that he and his fellow dark angels had made sure Marcus had gone away and that she was safe.

And he'd obviously kept up the charade in order to keep protecting her when she had been totally helpless, presumably in the emergency department of whatever this hospital was. He'd even gone an extra mile in giving her a new name so Marcus wouldn't be alerted to where she now was. Not just any name, either. He'd loaned her his own, along with the additional protection of allowing people to think she was his wife.

His *wife*.

Ellie took another look at this extraordinary man. He was a hero, no doubt about that. Maybe he wasn't wearing his motorbike leathers right now and he looked tired and unshaven but he was still absolutely gorgeous. And he was capable of bestowing the most beautiful smiles in the world.

The woman who would be his real wife one day was the luckiest woman in the world. She just didn't know it yet.

Gratitude for all that he'd done for her was filling Ellie's heart. Competing—no, meshing with the overwhelming love she already had for the tiny person she still held in her arms. It was all too much and it seemed to be getting hard to breathe again. So hard, it was utterly exhausting.

A pinging sound came from somewhere above her head and then there was the sound of footsteps approaching rapidly.

'Oxygen saturation level's way down,' a nurse observed. The alarm was silenced.

'Hardly surprising. First time she's been awake and it's been an emotional reunion for these two.'

'Of course it has. But I need to put some oxygen

on and she needs to rest. I think you'll have to take baby back to the PICU, Dr McAdam.'

'*No.*' The word was ripped out of Ellie in a gasp.

'Just for a while, Ellie.' Max's hands were moving under her arms already, preparing to lift the precious bundle. He was still bent over her. 'She's being taken good care of, I promise.' His mouth was so close Ellie could see every nuance of the words being made. 'She's safe, Ellie. Believe it and rest. We both want you to rest and get better.'

'Of course you do.' The nurse had a smile in her voice. 'Don't worry. I'll take good care of Mrs McAdam for you.'

Mrs McAdam?

This *was* a dream. Or maybe a nightmare, Ellie decided as Max took her daughter from her arms. But then he leaned in and kissed her. Softly, on her lips, and Ellie found her eyes drifting shut. This was most definitely a dream.

'Sleep well, darling,' he said clearly. 'I'll be back very soon.'

* * *

This time when Ellie woke her eyes snapped open and focused instantly. The wave of disappointment at finding the space beside her bed empty was enough to make her cry out.

'What's wrong?' The nurse was on the other side of the bed and Ellie could see a cotton bud in her hand as she turned her head. 'Sorry, I didn't mean to wake you but your lips were looking so dry and uncomfortable.'

'Where are they?' Ellie knew she sounded frightened but she *was*, dammit. She was alone apart from a nurse she didn't recognise. Was her baby alone too? Feeling unprotected and vulnerable?

'It's two a.m., Ellie,' the nurse said kindly. 'They'll be asleep. I expect your baby is safely tucked up in her crib and that Max is sprawled in the armchair beside her.' Her voice took on a wistful note. 'Or maybe he's holding her right now. He won't let anyone else feed her, you know.'

Ellie stared at the nurse. No, she didn't know and she didn't understand. 'But…it's been days,' she said finally, her voice wobbling. 'Days and days.'

'I know.' The nurse, an attractive blonde with a name tag that said 'Tori', took a deep breath and let it out in a sigh. Then she smiled at Ellie. 'We were all gobsmacked to hear that Max had got married secretly, but you know what's blown everyone away even more?'

Ellie shook her head slowly. So it hadn't been a dream. She had to pretend she was Max's wife for the moment. Oh…Lord!

'What an amazing father he's turned out to be,' Tori said. 'He was wearing his leathers when he came in with you, do you remember?'

Ellie found herself smiling. Oh…*yes*…

'I don't think he got out of them for the next thirty-six hours. He was sitting up there in the PICU doing kangaroo care. I've got a friend who works in there and she said that none of them could take their eyes off him. There he was, in those mega-masculine clothes, with a newborn baby skin to skin with him on his chest. Tucked under that leather jacket. Can you imagine?'

Ellie could. She remembered that jacket. And that chest. Maybe her contact had been very brief but she would never forget how solid it had felt. How safe. There'd been layers of clothes over it, of course but, oddly, it was all too easy to imagine how it might feel skin to skin. It gave her a sharp twinge in a painful place deep down in her belly. Painful but far from unpleasant.

She went back to picturing her baby and she knew how protected she would have felt and it was enough to bring tears to her eyes. She loved Max for what he'd done for her daughter. She would never, ever be able to thank him enough.

'He didn't have to keep it up for so long,' Tori continued as she poured water from a jug on the bedside table into a cup that had a built-in straw. 'A few hours at a time would probably have been enough to get all the medical benefits for the baby but he wouldn't leave her. He got his shifts in Emergency covered and stuff brought in from home. He's practically moved in.' Tori was smiling widely now. 'Not that any of the nursing staff are complaining, mind you. Would you like a drink of water?'

'Yes, please.'

'Just a sip to start with. Your tummy hasn't had anything in it for a while and I don't want you throwing up.'

Ellie sipped the cool water and it tasted wonderful. She drew in a deep breath. And then another. It felt easier.

'Any pain?' Tori queried.

Ellie thought about it. That was better too. 'I feel good...I think. Can I sit up? Or go to the loo or something?'

'You don't need to. You've still got a catheter in. I think they're planning on taking it out tomorrow and you might be able to have a shower, even. Word is that if you stay as stable as you've been today, they'll shift you out of ICU and onto the ward. The maternity ward,' the nurse added with another smile. 'You can have your baby right beside you. How good will that be?'

But Ellie was frowning as she remembered something Tori had said earlier. 'Why is she in the PICU? Max said she was fine.' Her mouth trembled. 'He said she was p-perfect.'

'She is,' Tori assured her hurriedly. 'On the small side, but there's nothing wrong with her. She went there initially because she needed watching but now it's more like staff privilege, I guess. It was a private space for Max to do the kangaroo thing. I think he might have been a bit embarrassed to be seen bonding with his baby like that, you know?' She chuckled. 'Men, eh?'

'Mmm.' Of course he would have been embarrassed. It wasn't even *his* baby.

What on earth had made Max go this far to help her? A total stranger. He had to be the most extraordinary person she'd ever met. Never mind how lucky his future wife would be. *She* was the lucky one right now.

'Would you like a bit of a wash, seeing as you're awake? I could help you clean your teeth.'

'That would be wonderful.'

'And then you can catch some more sleep and when you wake up in the morning, I'll bet your family will be back in here.' Tori paused as she headed off for supplies. 'Have you guys got a name for the baby yet?'

'No…I kind of expected it would be a boy.'

A boy that she would always have worried might turn out to be like his father. But what had Max said? That her baby might be a girl and pretty, just like her mum.

Max thought she was pretty? Ellie could feel the flush of warmth in her cheeks.

'You're looking so much better.' Tori sounded satisfied. 'And there's no rush to come up with a name. Legally, I believe you've got a month before she has to be registered.' She grinned. 'Her dad started calling her "Mouse" and everyone else is now. Mouse McAdam. Bit different, anyway.'

Yes. Different. Untraceable.

Safe.

The end was in sight.

It should be a huge relief. It was a huge relief.

'How 'bout that, Mouse?' Max looked down at the bundle he was carrying in the wake of the nurse who was pushing the plastic wheeled crib. 'You're going to the maternity ward. Your mummy's so much better that she's going to be able to look after you now. How good is that?'

It was very good. Excellent, even. He would be able to go home and get a full night's sleep. He'd be able to get back to work and he couldn't wait for a full-on, exhausting shift in the emergency department. The last few days had been an unexpected and disturbing disruption to his life and the sooner it was back on track the better. Maybe he'd suggest a weekend bike ride to the guys. Rick might stop laughing at him, finally, for playacting being a father. Jet might stop glaring at him and muttering under his breath about how crazy he was.

They were almost there now. Ellie had been put in a private room at the end of the ward. She'd only been on her feet for the first time that morning and was so weak she'd need constant help for the next few days but the nursing staff would be there for her. It was what they were paid to do, after all, and they'd do it well because everybody fell in love with Mouse.

The weight in his arms was so familiar. The kangaroo care wasn't needed any more, of course, but Max would never forget the feel of that tiny body against his own. Or the moments of a satisfaction like no other he'd ever experienced. Like when he'd got her to take the bottle that first time. Or when she had only stopped crying when a nurse had placed her back in *his* arms.

'Here you go,' she had said, clearly reluctant. 'It's her daddy she wants.'

Daddy.

Was this what it felt like to be a father? He'd

known what level of responsibility it would come with. And the kind of background anxiety that something bad could happen that had led to an urge to protect that was very disruptive to say the least. It had been crazy, hadn't it, to take time off work to guard this infant? And if he'd felt this strongly about a baby that wasn't even his, heaven help him if he ever got one of his own. If anything, he could take this whole experience as a warning.

The baby didn't seem to approve of being re-located. She was whimpering by the time they reached the room where Ellie was sitting, propped up on pillows. She looked pale and her long hair lay in limp, dark strands but the IV lines and the oxygen mask had gone and when she saw Max coming through the door, carrying her baby, her face lit up with a smile that made him catch his breath at its brilliance.

She held out her arms and Max handed over the bundle. He hung around, though, because Mouse was crying and, well, he might be the only one who could settle her down properly. He knew this baby better than anyone, including her mother. They might need him. Just for a bit longer.

The staff busied themselves.

'She's hungry,' a nurse declared. 'I'll go and fix a bottle for her.'

Max nodded. She *was* hungry, he could recognise the cry. He couldn't leave yet because he'd be able to help Ellie with her first feed. He was good at bottles. He knew just how Mouse liked it to be held and how far to tip it and when. How you knew it was going well because her eyes would find yours and stare at you with that intense concentration that made you feel like the most important person in the world.

'I…I thought I'd try feeding her myself,' Ellie said.

She must have noticed his expression because a faint blush spread over her cheeks.

'I'm drug-free, and the midwife who came to see me this morning showed me how to express milk and she said it hasn't dried up and there'll be plenty once I start feeding. And if there isn't…' Ellie sounded a little defensive now. 'I can top up with a bottle but it's going to be good for both of us if I give it a try.'

'You want some help getting her latched on?' the nurse queried.

'Um…I'd rather try by myself.' Ellie ducked her head, embarrassed. 'The midwife gave me the *Don't Panic Guide to Birth* to read and it's great. There's a technique in it that should work just as well for a baby this long after birth as if I'd done it straight away.'

'I've read that.' The nurse nodded. 'It's about being skin to skin and letting the baby latch on by itself, isn't it?'

Ellie nodded, shy but eager.

'That's supposed to be between the mother and baby, unassisted, but…' The nurse was frowning. 'Given that you've just come from the intensive care unit, I'm not happy leaving you entirely by yourself with baby.'

Mouse was crying in earnest now, sounding

distressed, with a warbling cry Max hadn't heard before. It was making *him* feel tense.

'Maybe if the father stays,' the nurse suggested. 'That's allowed, isn't it?'

Ellie was rocking the baby. 'Shh, shh…' she crooned. 'It's all right…'

Except it wasn't all right. Max could see his own tension in Ellie's face and hear it in the escalating misery of the baby's cry. Someone needed to sort this out.

'Of course it's allowed,' he snapped. 'Why wouldn't it be? Might be a good idea if you all left us to it.'

They went, closing the door behind them. Max drew the curtains over the windows on the corridor side of the room.

'What should I do?'

'Nothing,' Ellie said. She was peeling away baby blankets. 'I need to undress…her.' She was fumbling with the ties on the baby's gown but then she looked up and Max could see the tears in her eyes. 'She hasn't even got a name,' Ellie choked out.

'Yes, she has.' Max stepped closer. He knew how to take that gown off. 'She's Mouse. Because she's tiny and cute and sometimes she twitches her nose. Do you need the nappy off as well?'

'I…I don't think so.'

'Skin to skin, right?'

Ellie didn't meet his eyes. 'Mmm. I need to put her…um, Mouse, between my breasts.'

Max swallowed. 'OK. I'll hold her for a tick while you sort *your* gown.'

He was used to holding this baby when it was virtually naked. The movements of small, unfettered limbs no longer triggered alarm. He held the baby against his chest and, by some miracle, it calmed her. He could feel the rub of that tiny nose against his shirt and the high-pitched cries softened into noisy snuffles.

'She likes you,' Ellie said.

'She just knows me. Maybe it's a smell thing.' Max was busy not looking at Ellie as she took her arms from the sleeves of her gown and pushed it down to her waist.

'Mmm.' Her voiced sounded oddly strangled. 'That's what the book said. The baby needs to see and hear you and smell and taste. I put her face down between my breasts and stroke her back and she learns my smell and then she should start moving her head around until she finds the nipple all by herself.'

'Really?' Max was surprised enough to look up and there was Ellie with her breasts exposed. Small and round, like the rest of her. Pale and firm looking, with a tracing of blue veins and nut-brown nipples.

Max had to swallow hard again. He shouldn't be doing this. He really shouldn't. He could see the same discomfort in Ellie's eyes when he hauled his gaze away, a flush of something like guilt warming the back of his neck. For two pins he'd give her the baby and leave her to it but he couldn't do that, could he? They wouldn't let her do this alone and if she had a complete stranger watching, the chances of this going well might be greatly diminished.

So, instead, he smiled. 'You look like a Madonna,' he told her. 'You ready?'

'Mmm.'

Max had to position Mouse and that inevitably meant that his hands had to touch her breasts. He tried to ignore the awareness. The odd tingle it gave him deep in his gut. At least it didn't take long and then he could step back and simply observe. Be there in case Ellie needed rescuing.

It seemed to be going well. The baby stopped even snuffling as it lay there against its mother's skin. Ellie stroked her gently down the middle of her back and then raised her hand slowly to repeat the motion. Again and again.

So softly. Her fingers tracing a miniature spine. The movement had to be soothing.

It was certainly soothing Max.

Mouse was moving now, pulling her little legs up and then pushing them down again.

'Do you think she needs a blanket?' Ellie spoke in a whisper.

'It's pretty warm in here. See how she goes.'

The baby had looked up at the sound of Ellie's voice.

'She's watching me.' There was wonder in the whisper now.

Max watched Mouse. He saw her put her hands up to her mouth and then fling an arm sideways to make contact with a breast. She started to move her head from side to side, rubbing her nose on Ellie's skin the way she had been doing on Max's shirt not so long ago.

He opened his mouth to make an encouraging comment but then shut it again. He didn't want to break whatever magic was happening here. Voices and other noises from beyond the door faded into irrelevance and there was a silence in this room that had a very different feel to it. Both Max and Ellie were watching the baby, totally caught up in something they had no need to interfere with. Something primaeval and instinctive.

Something very wonderful.

Mouse was bobbing her head now. Then she stretched her neck and her whole head jerked so that it landed on top of Ellie's breast. With a tiny gasp, Ellie moved her hands to support the baby who had opened her mouth to poke out her tongue and lick the skin right beside a nipple.

Max held his breath. He could swear his heart stopped in that final moment when the baby's mouth closed over Ellie's nipple. And then he could hear the sound of sucking. When a tiny hand came up and pressed against the pale skin of Ellie's breast, he actually had to swallow past a constriction in his throat that felt horribly like tears were not far away.

Ellie looked up then and she had tears she wasn't bothering to swallow away. They rolled down her cheeks and her eyes shone with more of them but Max had never seen such an expression of joy in anyone's face. He couldn't look away. Couldn't swallow quite hard enough either but it didn't seem to matter that his own eyes got so wet.

This was a moment he would remember for the rest of his life. This joy. This connection. Between Ellie and her baby. Between Ellie and himself.

It made everything that had happened in this crazy week worthwhile because if he hadn't pretended to be the father of this baby, he wouldn't be here right now. He wouldn't have witnessed that little miracle of nature.

He and Ellie had shared the magic. No one else could be part of it or even begin to understand it. It was Ellie who finally broke that eye contact and he could sense what an effort it had taken. She looked down again. So did Max.

And there was Mouse. Sucking blissfully and staring up at her mother. Ellie wouldn't look up at him again. Max knew what it felt like to be caught in *that* gaze. He could blink away the moisture in his eyes now. Take a deep breath and let it out very slowly. He could even smile.

His work was done.

CHAPTER FIVE

'HAPPY birthday, dear Mouse… Happy birthday to you.'

Ellie was laughing. 'She's only a week old!'

Max was holding a bunch of rainbow-hued balloons. He tied them to the doorhandle and then ducked outside the room again. Ellie's jaw dropped when he returned moments later with his arms overflowing with parcels. He put them on the end of her bed where there was plenty of room because Ellie was sitting cross-legged, her back against her pillows and her baby in her arms, seemingly engrossed in being fed.

'Max…what have you *done*?'

The intent look she received from those dark eyes was out of kilter with the satisfied smile that was fading a little.

'You didn't have a whole lot of baby stuff ready, did you?'

'No.' Ellie bit her lip. 'I thought I had plenty of time and…and I had other things on my mind.'

The smile brightened again. 'I thought as much. And they're talking about letting you guys escape so I thought you'd need a few things to start you off.'

'Oh…Max…' It was embarrassing how easily tears came to her eyes these days. Ellie had never been one to cry much. 'As if you haven't done enough for us already.'

Max shrugged. He stepped closer and peered down at the baby. 'Is she done? Looks like she's asleep.'

'She is.' Ellie slipped her little finger into the corner of the tiny mouth to break any remaining suction. It also exposed her nipple to Max but any embarrassment over something like this had long since vanished. It had probably evaporated that very first time, in fact, when they had shared that amazing experience of Mouse finding Ellie's breast by herself.

'Maybe I could hold her for a bit, while you open her presents.'

'OK.' Max was the one person in the world that Ellie could hand her baby to without a qualm. He took Mouse and positioned her upright against his shoulder and he began rubbing her back gently.

Ellie opened a parcel to find a selection of tiny stretch suits in pink and yellow and the palest green. Another had tiny singlets and hats and one was full of bootees, including a soft yellow pair that looked like ducks. There were toys. Rattles and small, stuffed animals and a brightly co-loured play rug. Sleep suits that buttoned up like tiny sleeping bags at the bottom and even a dress that was a smocked white affair with a scattering of exquisite, embroidered flowers and a matching bonnet.

Ellie had to blink back tears yet again as she held it up. 'It's *gorgeous.*'

'I know it's probably a bit big but, hey…she's growing pretty fast.'

'Max…I don't know what to say.'

Mouse did. She gave an impressively large burp that made both Ellie and Max laugh and broke the potentially awkward moment.

Except that she had caught his gaze as they laughed and the eye contact held and became something else. Something huge that squeezed Ellie's heart so hard it was painful. It was Max who looked away first and she hurriedly dropped her own gaze and bit her bottom lip as the silence took on a heavier feel.

Max cleared his throat. 'I've been thinking,' he said.

'About?'

'You.'

Ellie's heart gave another squeeze and it was a noticeable effort to draw a breath.

'And Mouse, here.' Max had tilted his head so that his chin was touching the top of the baby's head.

'I know. I really have to decide on a proper name.' For some reason Ellie was feeling nervous now. What was Max about to say? Give her some last advice before disappearing from their lives? 'I'm thinking maybe Amelia? Or…or Charlotte?'

He frowned. 'Definitely not Amelia though I'm sure Jet would approve.'

'Why?'

'You know, Amelia Earhart? The famous female pilot?'

'Oh…' Jet had been up to visit once in the last few days and Ellie had had the impression he didn't approve of her at all.

'I wouldn't be in a hurry,' Max said. 'The longer it takes the better, really.'

'Why?'

'Because if you can't think of the right name, you won't be able to register the birth and the longer you leave that the better.'

'Mmm. I've been thinking about that myself. I'll have to use her real surname for that and if

Marcus found me because I bought a plane ticket, he might well be able to trace that.'

'Especially seeing as he had an idea of when the baby's due.' Max smiled at Ellie. 'Good thinking, having her a few weeks early. Gives you a bit of time to play with.'

'Except that I'll be registering her birth at about the time she was really due.'

Max nodded but he wasn't meeting Ellie's gaze. 'What if you could legally register her as McAdam?'

'You mean, change my name by deed poll or something?'

'No.' Max turned his head and his gaze locked with hers. 'I mean I could marry you.'

The world stopped turning for a heartbeat. Ellie had to close her eyes and then open them very slowly just to make sure she hadn't fallen into some parallel universe.

'Did…um…did you just say you could *marry* me?'

'Yep.'

'So that Mouse could have your name?'

'And you. You need a new name, too. It's not as if I'd be giving away anything I couldn't still keep myself as well. The perfect gift, if you put it like that.'

'Apart from ruining your single status.' Ellie's breath came out in a huff of laughter. 'I've seen the way the nurses around here look at you, Max. There's more than a few disappointed by your *pretend* marriage. A real one might take a lot more explaining.'

'Hey, am I complaining?' Max flashed her a grin. 'To tell the truth, I'm quite glad of an opportunity to be unavailable. Could be the making of me, being celibate for a while.'

'A while? That's like a piece of string, isn't it? How long were you thinking?'

Max looked serious again. 'As long as it takes, just like the string. How long do you think it will take you to settle into motherhood? Find a place you want to be and get your life on track?'

Ellie was silent. The future was huge and blank. The only goal she could focus on was to look after her daughter and keep her safe.

'Six months?' Max prompted. 'A year, maybe?' Still Ellie said nothing.

'Think of it like an insurance policy,' Max suggested. 'Think *about* it, anyway. The offer's there and I don't offer anything I'm not prepared to follow through.' He got to his feet and Ellie watched his hands as he shifted Mouse. One hand was under her small bottom and the other cradled her head to protect her neck. He moved her so gently she didn't stir in her sleep. 'I have to go,' Max said quietly. 'I'll leave you with the birthday girl but I'll be back later. We can talk about it when you've had a chance to think.'

Left alone, Ellie unwound her legs and climbed very carefully off her bed. She should put Mouse back into her crib to sleep but, instead, she found herself walking slowly around her room.

Thinking hard.

* * *

'You did *what*?'

The CT scan technician glanced sharply sideways at the two doctors standing in front of the screens that were about to show images of their patient's head and neck.

'We're almost good to go,' she said nervously. 'I'll just check on Stephen.' She ducked behind the glass screen to where two nurses were preparing a teenaged boy for the scan.

'I suggested that Ellie married me,' Max repeated patiently. 'It's no big deal.'

'Are you *kidding*? It's a huge deal. *Marriage?*'

'Keep your voice down. I'm supposed to be married to her already, remember? This would just make it legal as far as the paperwork goes. I'm talking name only. Ellie needs a new name. The mouse needs a name. I'm trying to make sure the poor kid doesn't end up being a "Jones".'

For once, Rick wasn't smiling. 'I suppose you're planning to put your moniker on the birth certificate, too?'

Max shrugged. 'I've gone this far. What's the harm in going a bit further?'

Rick whistled silently. 'The kid is going to grow up thinking that you *are* her biological father.'

'Not necessarily. I'm sure Ellie will tell her the truth when she's old enough to understand. It's not as though she'll remember me. I'm talking about a limited time, here. A few months maybe and then we'll get a quiet divorce. No harm done.'

'And fifteen years down the track? When a teenager you've forgotten about turns up on your doorstep because nobody got round to telling her the truth? What then?'

Max was silent for a moment. He wouldn't have forgotten about Mouse. No way. Rick cleared his throat as a prompt. '*I'll* tell her the truth.'

'Don't forget to tell your wife and the three kids of your own you'll probably have by then. Might throw a bit of a dampener on a peaceful evening at home otherwise.'

'I won't have a wife and three kids.' He could sound quite confident about that. Was it because the prospect was distinctly uninviting? An as-yet-unknown woman. Babies. Good grief, he'd been through more than enough in the last week to put him off babies for a very long time. Quite possibly for ever.

'What if it turns up with an adoptive mother?' Rick continued relentlessly. 'Like that Sarah who had your apartment? And they're there because you're the last hope to save the kid who desperately needs a bone marrow–transplant or a kidney or a bit of liver? How are you going to feel then? I'll tell you, mate. You'll feel like crap. Like you made a very big mistake a very long time ago.'

Max sighed. 'If you thought the worst-case scenario was going to happen you'd never do anything in life.' He wanted to change the subject. 'Like that kid in there. Stephen. He wouldn't have even started playing ice-hockey if he'd thought about getting tripped up and head-slammed into a wall.'

Rick gave a huff of laughter. 'Your logic's

flawed. You're supporting my side of the argument, here.'

Max ignored him. He looked at the technician who was still sending anxious glances towards the windows he and Rick stood behind. He pressed the microphone button. 'Good to go in there?'

She nodded and started the scanner. The bed began to move slowly into the mouth of the huge machine.

'We'll be right here, Steve,' Max heard her say reassuringly. 'Keep as still as you possibly can.'

A nurse ushered Stephen's frightened mother away. 'He'll be fine,' she was saying. 'It won't take long and his doctor's right here to watch him. He's got an expert from Neurosurgery to check the results as well. Try not to worry.'

The scanner whirred and clicked as it set itself into the programmed position to begin the scan. Rick's attention was on the patient file in front of him.

'Knocked out cold for approximately thirty seconds,' he read aloud. 'Retrograde amnesia, headache, repetitive speech and nausea. Sounds like a good going concussion.'

'Let's hope that's all it is,' Max said quietly.

'You've ruled out a C-spine injury?'

'X-ray looked OK. I wanted something a bit more definitive. Same with the brain injury. Watch and wait didn't feel right.'

'Gut feeling, huh?'

'Yeah.'

Just like his gut feeling that doing something extra was needed to protect Ellie and the baby. He knew it was crazy, dammit. He didn't need Rick chewing his ear off about it and heaven help him when Jet found out. He'd had second thoughts himself but if he'd learned anything in all his years of dealing with emergencies it was to listen to that gut instinct.

Sometimes, it saved lives.

Images began appearing slowly. Black and white maps of the interior of Stephen's body. So far, things were looking good. Maybe, this time, his gut feeling had been wrong.

'C-spine looks fine,' Rick pronounced.

'Mmm.' Just the brain to check now.

'Isn't Ellie due for discharge soon?' Rick asked as they waited for new images to appear.

The technician was seated at the far end of this bench under the windows and Rick was talking quietly enough.

'Yeah,' Max confirmed. 'Probably tomorrow.'

'Where's she going to go?'

The scanner was making enough noise to cover his response. 'It would look a bit weird if she didn't come home with me,' Max muttered. 'I've trumpeted the fact I'm involved, here. Anyway—' he knew he sounded defensive now '—I've got a spare room. It's no big deal.'

'You'll be living with her. She might find she likes it.'

Max said nothing. He thought about having company in his apartment. About coming home from work and finding Ellie and the mouse there. It wasn't beyond the realms of possibility that he might quite like it himself. For a while, anyway.

Wasn't a change supposed to be as good as a holiday?

'What if...?' Rick leaned closer. 'She decides she might like to be a *real* wife?'

'Not going to happen.'

'You mean you could live in the same house as an attractive woman and not take advantage of the situation?'

Max tried to shut down the mental picture of Ellie sitting on the bed that day, naked to the waist. He'd known the gut feeling he'd experienced then had been highly inappropriate. It was worse now. For God's sake, Ellie had just had a baby. Maybe the last time she'd been with a man had been when she'd been raped. This was sick.

And yet it hit him with all the force of a kick from a small mule. Suddenly Max was angry. With himself. With the situation he found himself in. Most of all, with the bastard who'd done this to someone like Ellie in the first place.

'Of course I can,' he hissed at Rick. Couldn't his friend see how far he was going in order to protect her? Suggesting he might try something that had the potential to hurt her was an insult.

'Hmm.' Rick was staring at the screens again. 'Good luck with that, mate.' His tone was distracted and Max focused on what his colleague was seeing. He knew the significance even before another one of Rick's silent whistles. 'Look at that. Your gut's on the money again. Subdural bleed…right there, see?'

Max could indeed. 'And another one there. Look. It's a coup-contrecoup injury.' The brain had bounced in the skull on impact and created an area of damage at both the front and back. 'Guess I'll be handing him over to your team, then.'

Rick nodded, still studying the images, any personal exchanges forgotten. 'Could well be heading for surgery. Good call, Max.'

Yes. Sometimes listening to that gut instinct could save lives.

What was Ellie's instinct telling *her* in regard to whether or not to take up his offer?

Would she say yes?

As crazy as it was, Max hoped she would. He just knew—for the same kind of inexplicable reasons that had made him insist on further investigations for his patient—that it was the right thing to do.

For everybody.

Had he been serious?

Marriage?

Ellie had no reason to think Max hadn't been serious given that he'd already claimed paternity of her daughter and given her the pretence of being his wife for the last week.

But this was huge. This would mean going through at least some form of a wedding ceremony with him to make it legal.

And that was wrong. Just so wrong.

She would say no, of course. He might be hugely relieved but he might ask her why not and what could she say to that?

That the offer was too over the top? Amazing? *Perfect?*

Except it wasn't and that was the problem. He wasn't talking about anything like a real marriage here. He was offering her the gift of his name so that she would be legally entitled to use it. It was an abuse of what marriage was and that cut too deeply to be acceptable to Ellie.

She'd grown up with a single mother and had dreamed of being part of a 'real' family for her entire life. It wasn't that she'd had an unhappy childhood, it was just that she had seen what others had had and had known there was something missing. And then she'd been given a stepfather when she'd been ten years old. He'd been willing enough to take on someone else's child but the truth that there was never any real connection there had become blindingly obvious when they'd had their own child a couple of years later. Despite her mother doing her best to ensure she was an integral part of the household, Ellie had always felt she was on the outside, looking in on a real family.

At some point in her teenage years, childish

fantasies of her real father turning up in her life had been abandoned in favour of her making her own family one day. Finding a man she could love with all her heart who loved her just as much. Having their own children. A home that was a *family* home. Full of laughter and love and the occasional smell of baking. A dog and maybe some hens out the back so she could collect her own eggs for that baking.

OK, so she'd messed up on part of it and the man who was the father of her baby was totally wrong but that didn't mean it had to be completely over, did it? She could make a home for her child. She could have the dog and even the hens, dammit. And one day she might find a man who would love her *and* her child. He would offer marriage and become a part of her family. Having to explain that she'd become pregnant by a man she didn't love would be bad enough. Telling him that she'd married the first time in name only would be even more shameful.

It would belittle something that meant the world

to Ellie. Make a mockery of her accepting a pro-
posal and saying vows that included 'till death us
do part'. She couldn't…*wouldn't* do it.

Was it fate that made Max appear at the very
instant she knew why she couldn't possibly accept
his offer?

'Hey…how's it going?'

Ellie smiled. 'All good. Very quiet. Mouse has
been asleep for hours and I've been enjoying the
view. I love how hilly Dunedin is.'

'It's a nice little town. I haven't been here that
long myself but I'm getting to know it. It's a good
place to live.'

'Mmm.' Ellie was trying to find the right way
to tell him that she wasn't going to be living here.

'I went past the office and had a chat to your
nurse. Looks like you'll get the all-clear for discharge after rounds tomorrow morning. You can
get out of here and go home.'

Ellie stared at Max.

Go home?

Where was that, exactly?

Most of her belongings were in storage in Wellington and all she'd come here with had been an overnight bag and her passport. If that became known it would ring alarm bells for the medical staff for sure. The kind of alarms that would set wheels in motion. Social service type wheels because they couldn't let a mother who was only just on her feet after a life-threatening event go off and provide sole care for a newborn baby.

And if she got sucked into that system there would be no hiding her real identity. Marcus would be able to trace her in a flash. He would turn up and she would be weak and vulnerable and wouldn't have Max or his friends to stand up for her. She could go further north to the town where her mother and stepfather were but they had a small house, two teenage boys and their own worries. Ellie hadn't even told them she was pregnant. Turning up on their doorstep with a baby was an option that was definitely a very last resort.

Max was watching her. 'You're going to need

help for a while yet, Ellie. You know that, don't you?'

Ellie nodded. 'I don't expect you to provide it, Max. I've got to start standing on my own two feet. This is my fault, because I didn't plan ahead. I was so busy taking it all one day at a time and relying on some airy-fairy plan that I would go and start a new life in a new place.'

'You can still do that. Just not tomorrow.'

The small squeak from the crib was a welcome distraction from having to face a reality that had very scary blank patches. Ellie reached into the crib and gathered her daughter into her arms, holding her close enough to bury her face against her body for a moment.

The rush of love she felt for this tiny creature was enough to bring tears to her eyes and feed a seed of determination. She had someone more important than herself to think about now. Someone she loved who would love her back. As she carried the baby to the towel on the bed in preparation to change her nappy, Ellie had a moment of clarity that was as welcome as the distraction had been.

It didn't matter that Marcus was her father. Maybe she would even thank him one day for being responsible for this incredible gift. Max had been right. Anything negative on the paternal side had most likely been due to nurture, not nature. This little girl was going to be brought up with the kind of love that would make her into a person Ellie knew she would be very, very proud of.

She was already. Taking hold of two tiny hands, Ellie bent to kiss her baby.

'Isn't she beautiful?'

'Yeah.' The word was gruff. Not that Ellie looked but she wouldn't have been surprised if Max had glanced over his shoulder to make sure no one overheard.

Not that she was fooled. He might have tried to hide it over the last few days, with that casual dropping in to see how things were going, but Ellie hadn't missed the sidelong glances into the crib or at the bundle in her arms. He might shrug as though it was unimportant when he was offered a cuddle but she hadn't seen him refuse one yet. And there'd been that time when Mouse had been crying and crying and Max had turned up and taken her and she'd snuggled in to his chest and settled.

There'd been more than satisfaction in the look Max had bestowed on the baby he'd held and the look had gone on for long enough for Ellie to recognise it as the kind of connection she had found in breastfeeding. And what about that shower of gifts for her one-week birthday this morning? She was wearing one of the tiny stretch suits now and Ellie eased the small legs out, bending again to kiss a miniature foot.

She hadn't known Max very long at all but she owed him her life and the chance to start again properly and she loved him for that along with everything he'd done since then. As a friend. She wasn't *in* love with him.

But she *could* be. Heavens, this was turning

into a series of revelations. Was it just that she was well on the road to recovery now and her brain was waking up? Yes. It would all be all too easy to fall in love with Max McAdam and what would that get her? A broken heart, that's what.

She'd seen the way women looked at him and knew why they looked that way. He was gorgeous and successful and she knew better than any of them how kind he was. He could have anyone he chose so why on earth would he be interested in someone as ordinary as her? Someone with someone else's child in tow, what's more, and she knew better than most what kind of heartache that could result in.

She didn't dare look at him for a minute. Just in case she found herself looking for something it would be very unwise to look for. Like the possibility that she was wrong. That there might be a scrap of hope that he *could* be interested. She needed a new distraction.

'She really does need a proper name,' she said, rolling up the dirty nappy to discard.

'That's what I came to talk to you about.'

Oh, help. As if she could get her head around explaining why she wasn't going to accept his offer of marriage when she was trying to suppress the knowledge of how easy it would be to fall in love with this man.

'I meant a first name. Can't see myself enrolling her at school as Mouse.' Ellie tried to make light of changing the subject. Cleaning the small bottom in front of her was helping. 'It needs to be a special name, though.'

'What's your mother's name?'

'Joan.'

'Oh…' Max was watching as she put a clean nappy in place. 'That doesn't sound right.'

'No.'

'How 'bout your grandmother?'

'Beatrice.'

'That's not so bad.'

'Except that she disowned my mother when she became an unmarried mother.'

'Oh.' Was he going to make a comment about

history repeating itself? Ellie hoped not. 'There must be someone that's special. A name that you'd like to honour?'

Ellie looked up. 'Yes.' Her heart gave an odd little flip. 'You're right. There is. Someone I have no idea how to thank.' She smiled at him. 'I'm going to call her...Maxine.'

The look on his face was priceless. 'Are you *kidding* me? No. You can't do that. It's totally wrong for her.'

Ellie had picked up Mouse again. 'Maybe I was kidding about the name but I wasn't joking about having no idea how to thank you.' Suddenly the words fell into place easily. 'You've done so much for us, Max, and I can't believe you offered to marry me. I really appreciate the offer but I can't do it. It's...' He'd even given her words to borrow. 'Totally wrong.'

'But what are you going to do tomorrow?'

'Find a motel, I guess. Just for a week or two until I've got myself sorted out properly.'

Max shook his head. 'No way. You're not a hundred per cent yourself. I won't let you do that.'

'This is my life, Max,' Ellie said gently. 'My responsibility. You can't stop me doing what I want to do.'

'Wanna bet?' Max could feel himself scowling at her. 'I'm a consultant on staff here. You think they won't listen to me when I tell them you have nowhere to go that's suitable for a convalescent mother and a neonate?'

Ellie was biting her bottom lip. Mouse was rubbing her nose against her T-shirt and making noises that emphasised her need for some dinner.

'I'll have to go to my mum's, then.'

'And where's that?'

'A little town near the bottom of the Coromandel peninsula. Couple of hours by bus from the airport.'

Max shook his head. 'You can't travel that far yet. You've had adult respiratory distress syndrome, Ellie. Your lungs still need time to recover properly. Flying anywhere is out of the question.'

He wasn't sure it was contraindicated but delivered in such a decisive tone, it certainly sounded plausible and it should work as a means of preventing Ellie just getting on a plane and vanishing from his life.

What are you doing? The small voice in his head sounded astonished. Wasn't this the perfect way out? He could almost hear Rick and Jet applauding the voice but Max was determined to argue. She wasn't going to marry him and that was fine. Oddly disappointing but probably for the best given the kind of potential unseen complications Rick had enlightened him with. But to just vanish into nowhere? Not acceptable because…because…

'How did Marcus trace your whereabouts last time?'

Ellie went pale. 'OK. No flying, then. I'll get a car. I've got enough money saved to keep us going for a while.'

'A three-day journey with a week-old baby? For goodness' sake, Ellie, what are you trying to prove? I've got a spare room and it's no big deal.' Max stalked towards the window and then turned, rubbing his forehead as he took a quick glance at the closed door. 'Look…I've gone out on a limb here and everybody thinks I'm your husband. That I'm Mouse's father. How's it going to look if word gets out that you don't come home with me? That this has all been some kind of fraud?'

Ellie was backing away from him, Mouse in her arms. She sank into the armchair beside the bed and for a long minute, as she arranged her clothing to put her baby to her breast, there was nothing but the hungry infant's cries. And then there was silence.

'I don't want people to know,' Ellie admitted quietly. 'I don't want questions being asked or…or social services or someone getting involved but… but I can't just come and stay with you, Max.'

'Why not?'

In the instant before Ellie averted her gaze, Max caught a flash of something.

Embarrassment, given the flush of colour in her cheeks now? No, that didn't make sense. She hadn't hesitated to start breastfeeding in front of him and why would she? They'd been through a far more intimate session that first time.

Something Rick had said rang in his head like a warning bell. Something about her wanting to be a 'real' wife. Oh...*hell*. Was Ellie attracted to him? That could certainly make things a bit awkward. He wanted to help, not set her up to get hurt. He wasn't offering to settle down and take on an instant family.

Perish the thought.

But he'd offered marriage.

What *had* he been thinking?

This was a mess. Max stared at Ellie's bent head, her hair falling like a screen to frame the baby, who was pushing on her breast with her little hand and staring up at her mother with a rapturous expression.

A warmth curled through Max. She was such a cute baby with her dark hair sticking up in spikes and eyes that still looked black. They'd got to know each other pretty well, him and the mouse. They were kangaroo buddies. And that gave him an idea.

'Ellie…we're friends, aren't we?'

She nodded. 'Of course. I owe you so much.' She looked up and her eyes shone with moisture. 'I'll never ever forget what you did for us.' Her smile was wobbly. 'A week ago you'd never met me. We don't know each other, really, do we? Not well enough to live together.'

They knew each other well enough, Max wanted to tell her. She knew he was looking out for them. He knew that she had been through a rough time and had the guts and determination to get through whatever life threw at her. But maybe she had a point. The offer of marriage had been misguided. Maybe living together, even temporarily, was also unwise.

'How 'bout a compromise, then?'

'Like what?'

'There's a motel about three doors down from

my apartment block. I could give my address for discharge details and take you to a unit there. That way, you'd be independent but I could drop in a couple of times a day to make sure you were OK and I'd only be a phone call away if you had any problems.'

'Y-you'd do that?'

'Of course.' Max nodded slowly. 'Hey…I told you you were safe, remember? You're not. Yet. You will be, but if you go steaming off on your own right now and something happens to you, or Mouse, how do think that would make me feel?'

Just terrible, he answered for her silently. Never mind fifteen years down the track like Rick had warned. He didn't want to feel bad tomorrow, thanks very much.

Ellie held his gaze and seemed to read the correct answer to his question. The tense lines in her face softened and she smiled.

'The motel would be perfect.'

CHAPTER SIX

THE motel was a long, long way from being perfect.

'I guess it's clean enough,' Max said, somewhat dubiously.

It was also completely without any character to give it warmth. Bland, white walls, grey carpet and tiles and no decoration other than a ghastly abstract print over the bed. There was a small couch, also grey, a television set and a kitchenette. An internal door opened to a bathroom that was as basic as the rest of the unit.

Max opened a cupboard beside a microwave oven. There was a single pair of everything. Two plates, two glasses, two cups and saucers. The cutlery drawer was just as sparsely furnished. He made a less than impressed sound.

'It's fine.' Ellie was sitting on the end of the bed,

holding Mouse. She looked pale and tired and no wonder.

'I shouldn't have made you stop at the baby shop. You look done in.'

'I just need to sit quietly for a bit. And I needed to go shopping. I couldn't have managed without getting the crib and nappies and everything.' She smiled. 'I'm glad you brought your car. I had visions of me leaving the hospital on the back of your bike.'

Max gave a huff of laughter. 'As if! The bike's a toy since I grew up a bit. I'll go and get the rest of the stuff.'

He went through the sliding glass door to where his SUV was parked directly outside. He had requested a unit near the manager's office for Ellie so that she had help nearby if needed it but also for security. Maybe it was better that she was here even if it lacked a little in material comforts. Marcus Jones knew where his apartment was and if Ellie was there, she'd be alone a lot of the time while he was at work. At least here she had the manager in residence and other patrons who would be coming and going.

It was just a shame it seemed so much more second rate in the daylight. He hadn't noticed how much traffic noise you could hear from the main road last night, either. Still…safety was paramount. He pulled the large, basket-style bassinette from the back of the car, throwing in the packs of disposable nappies and other purchases. A door slammed overhead and then a man's angry voice drowned out the traffic noise.

'Don't blame me, woman.'

'Don't blame *you*?' The female voice was shrill. 'It's *your* fault I'm stuck in this scummy motel with three kids. It was you and your drunken mates that got us evicted. It was you and your noise that made the neighbours complain.'

'*My* noise?' Max looked up in time to see the man kick the wall of the upstairs unit. 'Can you hear *yourself*, you stupid cow?'

From somewhere behind the woman came the

cry of a frightened child. The man swore loudly and turned his head, to see Max looking up.

'What are *you* looking at?'

Max simply stared back, saying nothing. He noted the tattoos and the piercings. The hunted expression on the face of a man who was far too young to have three children and housing problems. With another oath, the angry man took off, heading for the metal stairway at the end of the block.

'If you're going to the pub,' the woman yelled after him, 'don't bother coming back, you hear me?'

Max took the bassinette inside. Ellie had heard her, judging by the flicker of dismay in her eyes.

'You sure you want to stay here?'

She nodded. She even smiled. 'It's only for a week or two. I've coped with worse.'

Good grief, she was a determined soul and good on her. She'd need her courage and determination to be a good single mum and she would be good, Max was quite confident of that. She would be the best and Mouse was a lucky kid. He made one more trip to the car to get Ellie's bag.

'And you're sure you don't want the daily midwife visits? I'm not sure we did the right thing saying they weren't needed.'

'It would have been a bit tricky to have her visit the motel when you put your address down for me on the discharge papers.'

'Hmm. I forgot to tell you I registered you here under my name, too. I told the manager you were my sister.' Max was still bothered by the dismissal of the home visits most new mothers relied on. It was supposed to be getting less complicated to maintain the deception now that Ellie was back in the real world. He had to get rid of this gnawing sense of responsibility.

'How will you know if Mouse is getting enough milk without her getting weighed every day?'

'She won't sleep if she's hungry. I've got the bottles and formula if I need it and I've got the outpatient appointments for us both in two days. We'll be fine, Max, honestly.'

'Well, I'm only a phone call away, don't forget. I'll be working for the next few days to make up for the time I took off last week but it's day shift. I'll pop in on my way to work if it's not too early for you and I'll come again on my way home. I can bring you some takeaways so you don't have to worry about cooking.'

'You don't—'

Max overrode her intended objection. 'What kind of food do you like? Chinese? Indian? Burgers?'

Ellie conceded defeat graciously, with a shy smile. 'Fish and chips. I haven't had any for ages.'

'There's a little shopping centre just round the corner on the main road. About five minutes' walk, I guess. It's got milk and bread and all the basic stuff. Make a list and I can run down and get the things you might need for the rest of today.'

Ellie wasn't about to agree to any more assistance. 'A five-minute walk won't be a problem. I'll get sorted here and have a rest and then I'll try out that baby sling I bought and take Mouse for her first outing.'

It was ridiculous to feel like he was being excluded from something important. What did he want? To accompany Ellie and Mouse to the shops so that people would think it was his baby? So he could feel some kind of fatherly pride?

This had to stop.

'I'd better get back to work. My couple of hours' cover for this morning has about run out. Text me if you need anything other than fish and chips when I'm on the way home. You've got my mobile number?'

'Yes.' Ellie was smiling again. 'Go, Max. You're needed at work.'

Meaning he wasn't needed here?

This was good. One step closer to discharging the responsibility he'd taken on when Ellie had stepped into his life.

Max went. Quickly. Before he had time to

register any more inappropriate reactions let alone try to analyse them.

Ellie watched the SUV pull away, leaving the space in front of her unit empty.

It felt empty inside, too. She was alone with her baby. Really alone this time. No bell to push to summon assistance. No medical staff walking past her door at frequent intervals or the familiar, safe sounds of a busy hospital.

Max would be back later, though, and Ellie was determined to show him how well she could cope. That she was worth the effort he'd already put in to helping her.

For the next few hours, Ellie coped very well. She arranged her things in the unit, which made it feel more like her own space. She made up the bassinette with the cute sheets that had little, yellow ducks embroidered on the edges. She arranged baby clothes in a drawer and positioned nappies and wipes beside the padded change mat. When Mouse woke up, she fed and then washed her, putting her into a new set of her birthday clothes. She took her daughter around the unit, telling her about every item of furniture and what grown-ups used them for and when she fell asleep again, she was happy to go into her new bassinette and Ellie flopped onto the big bed and slept deeply for some time herself.

She was woken by the sound of a television set coming on loudly next door. For a moment, she lay totally bemused by where she was and desperately wanting to simply roll over and go back to sleep but then she remembered and staggered into the bathroom to splash water on her face, hoping to wake herself up properly before Mouse needed attention or, worse, Max turned up with dinner.

The cold water didn't seem to help much. Ellie's legs felt like lead, her eyes were gritty and her brain distinctly foggy still. She pushed damp strands of her fringe out of her eyes as she dried her face. She was well overdue for a haircut. Maybe she should just chop it all off because finding the energy to brush it right now was just too hard. Dropping the towel, Ellie raised her gaze wearily to the mirror to consider the option.

Oh…Lord, she looked *awful.*

She'd lost a lot more weight than she should have by giving birth, thanks to being so ill for several days. Her face looked pale and pinched. Her hair was lank and the oversized sweatshirt that had been useful in helping disguise her pregnancy was totally swamping her now. She looked like a street kid. A homeless person. About as far from a competent new mother as it would be possible to look. It was a pathetic picture and, for a long moment, Ellie was swamped by more than the sweatshirt.

She *was* homeless. The future was a chasm of the unknown. She wasn't even here under her own name and she couldn't afford not to hide her existence. Until she escaped the country she was going to be afraid of discovery. Terrified of Marcus tracking her down. Of something happening that might separate her from her precious baby.

A door slammed upstairs and the sound of angry pounding began again. The wail of a siren could be heard from the main road advertising the urgency of some emergency situation. The tension was contagious. In a sudden panic, Ellie dashed from the bathroom. How could she have left Mouse unattended, even for a moment? Had she even locked the sliding door before she fell asleep?

Her heart pounding, she stood by the bassinette and looked down at the peaceful, innocent face of the sleeping baby. She had to fight the urge to snatch Mouse up into her arms so she hugged herself tightly instead.

Huge, hot, painful tears rolled down her face.

She wanted to be somewhere else. She wanted to feel healthy and full of energy. She wanted, more than anything, just to feel *safe*. To know that her baby was safe.

She wanted…Max.

Nothing felt this bad when he was close. He gave her strength. Made her feel…too much. Alive. Optimistic. *Safe*.

As if to underline the difference in the space she was in without Max, the noise overhead increased. There were crashing noises, an ominous moment of silence and then a cry of pain. A moment later, simultaneously, came a woman's scream and a large, dark shape hurtled down past Ellie's glass door.

The screaming continued but, by some miracle, it wasn't waking Mouse. Ellie ran to make sure her door was locked but, when she tugged the net curtain aside to expose the doorhandle, she gasped in horror.

The dark shape hadn't been a piece of furniture being tipped over the balcony, as she'd assumed. Sprawled exactly where Max had parked his car earlier was the body of a man, one jeans-clad leg at an awkward angle and a heavily tattooed arm bent under his head. Ellie could see the manager running from the motel office. The older man stopped and stared, his jaw sagging. The woman upstairs was still screaming.

The scene looked frozen. The man on the ground wasn't moving. Neither was the motel manager. Ellie yanked her door open.

'Call an ambulance,' she shouted at the manager. 'And the police.'

'*No-o-o…*' The screaming upstairs morphed into words. 'It was an *accident*. I didn't mean to… Oh, my God…*Nigel…*' Ellie heard the footsteps of the woman as she ran along the balcony to the stairs, sobbing now. 'You're not dead. Please don't be dead…'

Was he dead? Ellie's blood ran cold. She didn't want to be here with her innocent child with a dead man outside their door. The motel manager had vanished back into his office, presumably to call the emergency services. Other people were emerging from their units but they all looked unsure of what they should do. Maybe she was the only person here who had any medical training.

With a desperate glance at her sleeping baby for another heartbeat, Ellie stepped through her door and pulled it closed behind her. The least she could do was make sure the man had a patent airway and to keep his C-spine protected for the few minutes it might take for an ambulance to arrive.

'Hello…' She crouched beside the sprawled figure and touched his shoulder. 'Can you hear me?'

She hadn't expected a response. Falling from the second floor onto concrete was a recipe for a severe head injury and spinal trauma, if not instant death. Carefully, she tilted his chin just far enough to ensure his airway was open and then she bent, her cheek close to his mouth to feel for a puff of breath, her fingers on his neck to feel for a pulse and her eyes watching for any chest movement.

The woman was beside her now, sobbing uncontrollably as she dropped to her knees.

'Don't touch him,' Ellie warned. 'We don't want to move him in case he's got spinal injuries.'

'He's dead,' the woman sobbed. 'I killed him. Oh...*God*...'

'He's not dead. He's breathing quite well and he's got a good pulse.' She looked up at the gathering crowd. 'Can someone find a blanket, please? And maybe some towels? And check that an ambulance is on the way.'

'It's coming.' The motel manager appeared again. 'They'll be here as soon as they can.'

'Good. Can you put your hands on his head, like this...?' Ellie showed him how to support the man's neck. 'Keep him as still as you can. When we get a towel I'll make a padding to help. I'm going to check for any bleeding.'

Someone ran towards them with a pile of towels and some plastic shopping bags.

'I couldn't find any gloves,' the middle-aged woman said breathlessly, 'but I did a first-aid course and they said bags were good.'

'Thanks.' The word was heartfelt. Ellie hadn't

thought enough about her own safety. She put bags over her hands and a heartbeat later one was covered in blood. The man was bleeding heavily from a wound on the underside of his arm. Ellie turned the limb and a spurt of blood from a large laceration made it obvious an artery was involved. She covered the wound with her hand and pressed down hard. The rest of her survey would have to be visual. She couldn't see any more blood but there was an obvious, open fracture to his ankle. She needed something to cover it to help prevent infection. The man needed covering as well. If he was going into shock he needed to be kept warm.

'How did it happen?' someone was asking in a horrified tone.

'I saw him having another fight with his missus,' another voice answered. 'She went at him with something and he kind of rolled over the balcony railing.'

'Probably a knife, by the look of that arm. Has someone called the cops?'

'They're on the way.' The motel manager sounded grim.

'They've got kids, haven't they? Maybe someone better check on the poor little blighters.'

The woman had buried her face in her hands and was rocking back and forth, crying hysterically.

'Mummy?' A frightened voice came from overhead. 'What are you doing? Darren's crying. He's scared…'

Ellie glanced up to see the terrified face of a small girl who was crouched down and peering through the railings. It was a stark reminder that there were children involved here. She couldn't afford to forget about her own child either. Mouse was due to wake up any time now and the thought of her being alone in the unit and crying for *her* mother was unbearable. But she couldn't leave. She had pressure on an arterial bleed and she couldn't let go.

The voices of the people surrounding her began to blur into a muttering that merged with the wailing of the distraught woman and the cries of the children upstairs. Ellie's fingers in the plastic bag slipped for an instant and a fresh well of blood appeared. It made her feel faint. Dizzy.

And then she felt a firm touch on her shoulder. She knew it was Max well before she heard his voice. She could feel his presence. Solid and commanding. The dizziness faded.

'Hang on for a tick,' he said, close to her ear. His voice rumbled into her body and she could feel the awful tension retreating. 'You're doing great. I've got gloves here in my pocket.' He was pulling them on as he spoke. 'OK. I've got this.'

He crouched right beside her, close enough for his thigh to be pressed against her hip. A solid rock of a man. His hand pushed hers aside as he slipped it into position to apply pressure to the wound.

'Arterial bleed?'

'Yes.'

'Head injury?'

'Presumably. He's been unresponsive since he fell.'

'Fell?' Max flicked a gaze upwards. 'Good grief...anything else you've noticed?'

'Compound fracture of his tib/fib. I haven't moved him to check his chest or abdomen because I was worried about his C-spine. Breathing was OK. I've been kind of stuck with this bleed...'

The sound of an approaching siren was abruptly cut off. Flashing blue and red lights appeared over the heads of the crowd of bystanders as the ambulance backed in past the motel office.

'Make some room,' someone yelled. 'The paramedics are here.'

Max caught Ellie's gaze. 'You OK?'

Ellie wasn't at all sure about her emotional state but he was probably asking about her physical shape. She nodded.

'And Mouse?'

He must have seen the flash of panic in her eyes. 'Go inside,' he directed, turning his gaze to the paramedics who were climbing out through the open back doors of the ambulance. One carried a large, soft backpack of gear. The other held an oxygen cylinder in one hand and a lifepack in the other. 'We'll take over now. Hey…' He obviously recognised the crew. 'Good to see you guys. This chap apparently took a tumble from the balcony up there. GCS of three and I'm sitting on an arterial bleed here.'

Ellie edged back as the paramedics moved in.

'Grab a collar,' one told the other. 'And a scoop stretcher.'

She slipped through her door, not pausing until she stood beside the bassinette. The light had faded fast while she'd been outside and she had to blink for a moment to readjust. Because it was quiet in here, she had assumed Mouse was still asleep but her heart skipped a beat when she realised that the baby was awake. Not crying but staring up at her mother. She could imagine she saw recognition in that intense gaze. Trust. She hadn't been afraid because she knew that the person who loved her the most was coming back.

Ellie swallowed hard. She found a smile. 'Everything's going to be OK,' she whispered. 'Max is here. Let me just give my hands a quick wash and then I'm going to pick you up and I'm not going to let you go, I promise.'

With Mouse in her arms a short time later, Ellie went to stand in her doorway to watch the ambulance crew working under the direction of the emergency department consultant. They had a collar in place and an oxygen mask covering the man's face. IV lines were in and the motel manager was holding a bag of fluid aloft. A pressure bandage was in place on the lacerated arm and a splint was being applied to the broken ankle.

The police were here as well. A female officer went upstairs to the children and another two officers were taking charge of the woman, who had stopped crying and now looked so stunned she was making no protest at being led away.

The scoop stretcher was made ready to use. The paramedics then adjusted the man's position slightly so that he was completely on his back with his spine correctly aligned. It wasn't quite dark out there yet so there was more than enough light to see what had been hidden on one side of the man's lower chest.

A knife handle was protruding. Had he been stabbed before he'd fallen or had he been holding the knife and fallen onto it? Either way it was shocking.

The paramedics went into action smoothly and swiftly. They made a doughnut-shaped padding to go around the impaled object and stabilise it.

'Let's load and go,' one of them ordered.

'I'll leave you to it. He's looking stable.' Max stepped back as they clipped the scoop stretcher into place on either side of the man. He looked up as they lifted it and his gaze went straight to Ellie, standing there with Mouse in her arms.

The crowd shifted as the stretcher was carried to the ambulance. People wanted to see the end of this drama with the ambulance departing, hopefully with its lights and sirens activated. The police cars would be going soon, too, taking the woman and children away.

Max didn't go with them. He stripped off his gloves and dropped them onto the considerable pile of wrappings and other debris the paramedics had left behind. Then he walked straight towards Ellie. His face was grim. So was his tone of voice.

'Pack your stuff,' he ordered. 'There's no way you're staying here. I'm taking you home.'

CHAPTER SEVEN

'She can't go.'

'Excuse me?' Max flicked his gaze up from where he was slotting the bassinette, stuffed full of baby clothes and nappies, into the back of his car.

'Your sister,' the motel manager said nervously. 'The police might want to talk to her again. She's their best witness.'

'She's already given them a statement. They can talk again later. Preferably tomorrow. We're only going to be just down the road. I gave you my address on the registration form.'

The manager looked bewildered. Things were happening in his establishment that were far more than he had any desire to cope with. Max took pity on him.

'I know it's a bit weird. She should have come

home with me in the first place but she's kind of independent is my sister. Extremely capable but she likes to manage things on her own.' Not that she was putting up any kind of resistance to him having taken control for now. Ellie was sitting in the back seat of his car, with Mouse in the baby seat strapped in right beside her. She had to be listening to this exchange but she was sitting very still. Looking tense enough to snap at any moment.

Max didn't want any further delays. He smiled at the manager and lowered his voice. 'She doesn't really approve of me, you know? I like to ride motorbikes and have parties. Not the best environment for a new baby, is it?'

'N-no, I guess not.'

Max shut the back hatch of the SUV so that Ellie couldn't hear him. 'But this hasn't turned out to be a very good environment either, has it? I can't leave her somewhere where people get stabbed and thrown off balconies.'

'Nothing like this has ever happened before.'

The manager was almost wringing his hands. 'All the police here…all that blood… They're putting up tape, did you see? In case that guy dies and it becomes a crime scene. What's *that* going to do to my business?'

Max had seen the tape. Luckily he'd moved so fast he'd got most of Ellie's possessions out of the unit before it became impossible to access the door. Now he needed to get her away from here. The last thing Ellie needed was the police asking too many questions. They would be wanting to talk to him at some stage and *he* needed to think about what he was going to tell them concerning his relationship with their chief witness.

Talk about weaving a tangled web of deception. The strands were winding themselves ever more tightly around him and it was getting hard to think straight. All Max could do was run on instinct and hope that it served him as well as it always had when it came to out-of-control situations. He wasn't at all sure that it had worked particularly well over the last week but he had no choice other than to continue to go with it. No way could he leave Ellie here to fend for herself. She was in a fragile state anyway and this nasty incident must have shaken her up badly.

Max ignored the manager's anxious fluttering around the back of his vehicle as he climbed into the driver's seat. He had to manoeuvre to get out through the extra police cars that had arrived on scene and a glance in his rear-view mirror showed the manager now talking animatedly to an officer, pointing at his departing car. He suppressed a sigh. How much time would they have before someone official came knocking at his door?

For a wild moment, Max considered driving right past his own address. Finding somewhere else to put Ellie and Mouse. Somewhere nobody could find them. The police *or* Marcus Jones. But then what? They'd be totally dependent on him, wouldn't they?

And why on earth did that ridiculous scenario hold some kind of strange appeal? It was crazy. This whole week had been crazy and by the time

Max had formed that inescapable conclusion, he was outside his apartment.

'Here we are.'

The statement, admittedly uttered with some resignation, fell into silence. Max turned his head to find huge eyes in a very pale face.

'I'm really sorry, Max.' The apology was a whisper. 'I'm a lot of trouble, aren't I?'

Yes. She was. She and the mouse had turned his life completely upside down in the blink of an eye and the worst of it was that Max was still lying awake at night, haunted by what could have happened if he hadn't become involved. She'd got under his skin. Maybe it had happened in that first moment, when she'd stumbled into his arms and growled at him to let her go.

Or maybe it had been Mouse who'd really got under his skin. Seeped in, probably, which was hardly surprising when they'd spent so much time with their skins touching.

Whatever. He was in this up to his neck. He couldn't get out until that fierce Ellie appeared again. The one who would shove him away and growl at him in a brave stand for independence and autonomy. There wasn't a hint of fierceness in her face right now. Max could see fear and uncertainty. But when his gaze slid down and he saw her hand resting on the edge of the baby seat, holding a tiny hand in her fingers, he could see the bond between a mother and child. The love.

He could see the courage that came with that as a given.

And it was a gentle kind of fierce.

Max could only smile. A poignant tilt to his lips that felt nothing like any smile he'd ever produced in his life.

'Hey…' He moved his gaze back to Ellie's face. 'I like trouble. Keeps life interesting. They didn't call us the "bad boys" at school for nothing.'

He carried the baby seat into the apartment and then he ferried in the baby gear.

'Uh-oh…where's *your* bag, Ellie?'

'I must have left it behind. I was only grabbing baby stuff.'

'So you don't have a change of clothes or anything?'

'No.'

They both looked at what Ellie was wearing. The horrible, shapeless sweatshirt and jeans that looked five sizes too big. And then Max frowned.

'Your clothes are covered in blood.'

'Oh, my God…' Ellie stared down at her stained jeans. 'They're saturated. What if he had hepatitis? Or HIV?'

'Get them off,' Max said crisply. 'Get into the shower. Have a really good scrub. I'll throw these into the laundry and soak them in bleach. Check that you don't have any open wounds…on your legs, in particular. Did you get any blood on your hands?'

'No. Someone gave me plastic bags.'

'That's right. I wondered what you were using when I arrived. That's good.' Max stepped towards the baby seat where the mouse was beginning to squeak. 'I'll look after her. The bathroom's just down the hall. First door on the left.'

'But she sounds hungry.'

'I'll give her a bottle. She's had them before, I don't think she'll mind.' Max didn't mind either, he realised. He had enjoyed those feeding times up in PICU. Missed them, almost.

'But—'

He raised his eyebrows at Ellie as if surprised by her insubordination. 'Shower, Ellie,' he ordered. 'For Mouse's protection as much as your own.'

Ellie gave an audible gulp. 'But…I won't have any clothes.'

'I'll find you something and leave it outside the bathroom door. Go on. There are clean towels in there and plenty of soap and shampoo so wash your hair as well. A thorough scrub from head to toe, got it? Decontamination.'

He had undone the safety belt around Mouse and was lifting her into his arms. Ellie stood indecisively for a moment longer, watching him. And then, with a noise that could have been a tiny sob, she turned and fled towards the bathroom.

It was a good twenty minutes before she emerged. Her hair lay in damp strands over her shoulders, spikes of her fringe hanging into her eyes. She had rolled up the sleeves of that salmon-coloured shirt he rather liked even though it was too close to being pink and the tail hung down far enough to almost cover the red silk boxers he had also provided.

With her face scrubbed clean and her bare legs and feet, she looked like a teenager. A malnour-ished one at that. She also looked far shyer than Max had anticipated. She was in his house and now in his clothes and she was clearly discom-fited by the turn of events. She not only looked incredibly young but rather too vulnerable as well.

'Squeaky clean?' He tried to sound casual but he could *smell* how clean she was, dammit. Had she discovered some soap he didn't know he had? Or was that vaguely floral, gorgeously feminine scent simply coming from her exposed skin? He hadn't seen her this uncovered since that day she'd breastfed Mouse for the first time.

Oh, *God…* Why did that scene keep ambushing his brain, not to mention other regions of his anatomy?

Ellie was nodding. 'How did it go with the bottle?'

'See for yourself.' Max couldn't help a proud grin as he waved at where he'd placed the bassinette, tucking it into a corner of the living area, away from any draughts from the windows. 'Fed, burped, changed and back to sleep. I reckon she's had enough excitement for one day.'

The nod was heartfelt this time. 'Me, too.'

'Hungry?'

'Starving.'

'Me, too.' This was good. Something to focus on that took his mind off Ellie's bare legs and the knowledge that she wasn't wearing a bra under that soft, old shirt.

'The fish and chips are stone cold. I was just

waiting for you to get out of the bathroom so I could go and get a fresh lot.'

'*No.*'

Max stopped in his tracks even though he was already halfway to the door. Escape into some fresh air had been the perfect plan but the anguish in Ellie's whisper made him feel as though he'd come up against a brick wall.

'What's wrong?'

'I…um…I'd rather you didn't go. What if…the police come? What do I tell them?'

Her expression suggested a belief that Max would have all the right answers and her trust undid something deep within. So did the thought that she didn't want to be left alone. That she wanted *him* to stay with her.

'Oh…Ellie…' Her name was almost a groan. An admission of defeat?

He walked back towards her, one step at a time, feeling as if he had no other choice at all. He gathered her into his arms and then realised that this was the first time he'd held her since she had stumbled on his doorstep—a lifetime ago. She'd been covered in shapeless clothing then and all he'd really been aware of had been the baby bump between them. Now it was just Ellie with a mere layer of silky material between them. He could feel the real shape of her body and the way it fitted against his. The length of her back. Firm, round little buttocks, all slippery under the silk. Her nose was buried against his chest and it even rubbed against him, a bit like Mouse when she was hungry or upset.

Max held Ellie with one arm around her back and with the other he smoothed the damp strands of her hair.

'It's OK,' he heard himself murmur. 'I'll look after you. I'm not going anywhere for a while.'

The words seemed to echo. Where had he heard them before?

Oh…yeah… Back when he had started the skin-to-skin thing with Mouse, that's when. When he'd known he was caught for as long as it was going to take because to do anything else simply wasn't an acceptable option.

Ellie tipped her head back far enough to look up at him. Her face held a look of astonishment.

Of hope.

But a question lingered in her eyes. Was it possible he really mean what he'd just said?

Max couldn't think of anything more he could say to reassure her. Words seemed to have deserted him, in any case, as he looked down at those toffee-coloured eyes. At a nose that Mouse would undoubtedly share when she grew up. At lips that were parted just a fraction.

He tried to smile but that ability had clearly deserted him along with the power of speech. So he did something that seemed to come naturally. He bent his head and brushed her lips with his own. A kiss that wasn't really a kiss. Only reassurance. The kind you could give any female friend.

So why did it *feel* like a very different kind of kiss? The first stroke of something he wanted to dive into headlong. He was so aware of the scent of this woman in his arms. The feel of her body. He wanted to taste her. To hear the kinds of sounds she might make when she wasn't scared or shy. When she was more than merely happy, in fact. Max was good at eliciting sounds that came with intense physical stuff. A sigh of pure pleasure perhaps or the groan of ultimate satisfaction.

He could—

Whoa! Max managed to stop his mouth descending again. He even managed to straighten up. To suck in enough air to resuscitate his brain.

'How—'bout I put them in the oven, then?'

'Huh?' Ellie's eyes snapped open. When had she closed them? And *why*?

'The fish and chips. Would they be all right if we reheat them, do you think? I'd hate to give you food poisoning.'

'Oh…' Colour was flooding Ellie's cheeks and she wriggled free of his arm. Or maybe he'd dropped it already. 'I'm sure they'd be absolutely fine.'

'Right. I'm onto it, then.' Of course they'd be fine.

He would be too as soon as he was far enough away from the feel and scent of Ellie.

It hadn't been a kiss.

Not a real kiss.

It didn't mean anything. Not to him, anyway. To Ellie?

The world had tilted so sharply beneath her feet at the merest touch of his lips on hers that she knew she was in real trouble. She'd seen it coming, though, hadn't she? She'd known how easy it would be to fall in love with him. She'd tried, God help her, to maintain some distance. Just a shred of independence—both physical and emotional—and where had that landed her?

Here. In his apartment. In his clothes, for heaven's sake.

In love.

But just because you felt that strongly about someone it didn't mean you had to act on it, did it?

It didn't mean that Max was going to guess how she felt and run for the hills. And he would run. Why wouldn't he? He was a gorgeous bachelor, part of a group of them, and they all played with toys like powerful motorbikes and had women lining up for their attention.

Ellie couldn't afford for Max to want to run. She needed him right now. So did Mouse. They both needed his friendship and his protection. Not for ever. Just for a week or two. Surely she could keep the way she felt hidden for that long? And then she could step out of his life and keep the basis of a friendship that would last for a lifetime.

She had to try. Friendship with this man was an infinitely preferable option to scaring him off so that she never saw him again. They could stay in touch. Visit occasionally, even. It wouldn't be beyond the realms of friendship to ask him to be a godfather to her daughter and, that way, they would have a link for life. Not that she'd ask him just yet.

With their dinner reheating in the oven, Max

had taken himself off to a laundry space. He'd insisted that it was no trouble to disinfect Ellie's clothing and put it through the washing machine and dryer. It would be good to go in the morning. He'd been so keen, in fact, it had been difficult to avoid the impression that he found her wearing his clothes as disturbing as Ellie did, albeit for very different reasons.

He seemed to keep himself very busy for the rest of the evening as well. He made up the spare bed and helped Ellie sort the baby gear and then he made more than one phone call to speak to Jet, who was on duty again in the emergency department.

'That guy Nigel looks like he's going to make it,' he informed Ellie eventually. 'He's been to Theatre. The knife skated over his ribs and the damage was pretty superficial. His ankle's been fixed. He's got a good concussion but his C-spine checked out clear.'

'Oh…thank goodness for that. If it had turned

into a murder investigation, I would have had to stay in the country for court appearances or something, wouldn't I?'

Max gave her an odd look. 'Yeah…I guess. But you weren't planning on leaving immediately, were you?'

'As soon as I can.' Ellie found a smile to give Max. 'Don't worry. We won't be messing up your lifestyle for too long. We might even be able to go back to the motel tomorrow.'

The look she got now was almost a glare. 'I don't think so. Not with the type of clientele that place attracts. The police will be swarming around for days, I expect.'

'If Nigel's going to be all right, maybe they won't need to talk to me again,' Ellie said hopefully. 'I was worried about what to tell them.'

'The truth,' Max suggested.

Ellie's eyes widened. 'You mean my real name?'

'No, not that bit.' But Max looked less than sure. Then he gave his head a slight shake. 'It's not doing any harm,' he said. 'And it seems to be working so far. I'd stick to McAdam if I was you.'

Ellie had reason to remember the advice the next day, well after Max had gone to work and she was alone in the apartment with Mouse. She had her baby in her arms when the knock came at the door. For a moment, panic set in. It could be the police. It could also be Marcus. What if he'd had someone watching and had been informed that she'd moved in with Max? He'd had enough time to catch a plane from Auckland and find her here, without any protection other than a locked but probably flimsy door.

Heart thudding, she went to peer through the peephole on the door.

'Max?' A feminine voice called. 'You home, babe?'

The image through the peephole was distorted. Ellie could see what appeared to be the longest pair of legs she'd ever seen. Long and sleek and black. Like the hair that flowed from the woman's head. She opened the door and then wished she hadn't. The woman really was long and sleek. She towered above Ellie, thanks to the stiletto heels that finished the look of her tight leather pants. Ellie was back in her newly cleaned maternity jeans and baggy sweatshirt that had both gone a rather odd, patchy colour from being bleached. She had never felt so short and dumpy and dowdy.

'Ahh...' The woman's rapid up-and-down glance said it all. 'Is Max here?'

'No. He's at work.'

'Damn. I've got something I think he'll be quite excited about.'

Ellie didn't doubt that for a second. This woman would be just his type. Heavens, she already had biker chicks' pants on. She could sling a leg over the back of his bike and put her heavily bangled arms around his waist and ride off into the sunset at a moment's notice.

'I'm Gina,' the woman said. 'I'm a...friend of

Max's. And Rick's,' she added with a confident smile.

Ellie nodded. She tried, and failed, to smile back.

'And you are?'

It was right then that Ellie remembered the advice and it was simply too tempting not to use it.

'I'll Ellie McAdam,' she said.

'Oh…' Perfectly sculpted eyebrows shot up. 'Max's sister?'

'No.' This time, Ellie managed a smile. 'His wife.'

Maybe the advice hadn't involved using the fraudulent relationship as well as the name but Ellie couldn't resist. She couldn't even summon sympathy for how Max was going to explain his way out of this after she'd gone.

'And…' Gina's gaze dropped to the baby in Ellie's arms. 'Oh, my God…'

Ellie didn't say anything. She didn't need to.

Gina was obviously having no problem coming to her own conclusion.

'Um…' Her visitor had been holding something in her hands, which she now held out. 'I can see why he's on the lookout for a new property. This one might be really great for you guys.' Gina wasn't one to let an opportunity slip past, evidently. 'I met Max…and Rick at a bike show recently. I'm a real estate agent and Max gave me his details. Said he was on the lookout for a new property. This just came into the office and it's kind of special so, of course, I thought of Max.'

'Thanks.' Ellie's smile was genuine now. Sympathetic, even. She could well believe that Gina had thought of Max. What woman wouldn't?

Max didn't appear to have returned the interest, however.

'Gina? Gina who?' He'd brought Chinese food home with him and the aroma was seriously tempting as he unpacked the carry bags.

'She didn't say. Gorgeous looking, though.

Leather pants and long, dark hair. Said she met you and Rick at a bike rally or something.'

'Oh-h.… We did pop in on a Ducati show a couple of weeks back. Yeah…rings a bell. We swapped cards but I gave hers to Rick 'cos he was thinking he might give her a call.'

'She left you brochures. Said you were looking for a property to buy?'

Max grimaced. 'I should be but I really can't be bothered. I might just move back in with Rick when Jet gets another stint away with the army.'

'What's wrong with this place?'

'I've only got a sub-lease for three months. Sarah reckoned she wouldn't be away any longer than that, though I can extend it if she doesn't come back. She took this on as a two-year lease.'

'Oh?' Ellie was distracted, both by the tubs of hot food now on the table and the reminder of her old flatmate. 'I must email her and see how things are going with Josh.'

'Good idea. Might give me a shove in the right direction.'

'Which is?' Ellie pulled the disposable chopsticks apart. Max was opening the tubs and she'd never felt so hungry in her life. She must be getting better, she decided. Her body was coming back to life.

Max saw her practically drooling and he grinned. 'Good to see you looking hungry. Steak with black bean sauce in that one. This one's chicken and ginger and that's stir-fried veggies 'cos it looked healthy. There's a bucket of rice so dig in.' He dipped his chopsticks into the first container and started filling his plate. For a minute or two they were both preoccupied with their food but after a few mouthfuls Max paused and glanced at Ellie.

'I guess the right direction is settling down,' he said sadly. 'I'm thirty-six. I can't ride round on my bike and move from place to place for ever. I like it here in Dunedin so maybe I need to put some roots down. Buying a house seems like a good first step. What do *you* think?'

A settled-down Max? With a home of his own?

Would a wife and children and maybe even a dog be on the agenda as well?

Stupid to feel that bubble of hope but irresistible not to take the opportunity to soak in the expression on Max's face. To enjoy that rough look his jaw always had at this time of day that made her fingers itch to touch it. To make direct eye contact and feel it all the way to her bones.

'Couldn't hurt to look,' she offered. 'The picture's lovely and Gina seemed to think it was something special.'

'But it's way out on the peninsula. Long way to work.' Max ate in silence for a while again. 'Mind you, it's a great road for a bike ride. Good twists and turns and it runs right along the harbour's edge.' He ate another mouthful. 'I've got a couple of days off coming up. Why don't you come with me and help me look?'

'On your bike? Not on your life, mate.'

Max laughed, a wonderfully rich sound that made Ellie feel warm all over and happier than she could remember being in such a long time.

'Hardly. Not with the mouse to take into account. We'll take the car and it'll be as safe as houses, I promise.'

Ellie still shook her head.

'Why not?'

'Um…I kind of told Gina that I was your wife and she assumed that Mouse was yours as well. She looked kind of disappointed.'

Max was grinning. 'Is that so? I'll tell Rick. She's just his type.'

'Not yours?' Ellie knew she sounded surprised.

Max shrugged. 'Used to be. Maybe I'm growing up a bit. Thinking about house buying does that to a man, you know.'

Ellie wanted to ask what he thought his type was now but she didn't dare. This wasn't a conversation she really wanted to have because the little spears of wishful thinking were too delicious to want to give up. It couldn't hurt to indulge a small and very private fantasy for a little while, could it?

But Gina used to be his type and Ellie couldn't

help remembering the way she'd felt that morning. Dumpy and dowdy.

'I still couldn't go.' It was her turn to grimace as she looked down at herself. 'Even if I went back to the motel for my bag, I didn't bring any non-pregnancy clothes with me. I look like I've been rummaging through the unwanted stuff from a charity shop. You really wouldn't want to be seen out with me, Max.'

'So wear something else.'

'Don't think your boxers and shirt would work either.'

'So…go shopping.'

'What?' That hadn't even occurred to Ellie.

'You're feeling better, aren't you? You're certainly looking better.'

Ellie nodded.

'So, take a taxi and go to one of the big department stores in town. You could take Mouse in the car seat and they'd have everything under one roof. Not too much walking about to tire you out. You've got those outpatient appointments tomorrow afternoon, haven't you? So you have to go out anyway.'

Ellie continued to nod. Everything under one roof? Clothes, lingerie, shoes. A hairdresser, maybe?

How long had it been since she'd worried about her appearance? Or had a reason to want to look good? This was a kind of hope that was permissible. Part of her fantasy, maybe, but one that was grounded in reality. It could happen. She could make a dramatic improvement to the way she looked. It was exciting.

'If I go to a bank, I won't even have to use my credit card.'

'Is that a problem? You want some cash?'

Ellie shook her head hurriedly. 'I've just been careful for so long because people can trace where you are if you use cards, can't they? I've seen it happen on those crime shows.'

The reminder of why she had come here in the first place and the continued need for care dampened the atmosphere.

'I'm sure it'll be fine,' Ellie muttered. 'It's not as if he doesn't know where I am now anyway.'

He could be waiting. Biding his time. Probably quite confident that he would receive information about the birth of his child and he would, eventually, because time was running out. The birth had to be registered. Mouse had to be given a name.

'The offer's still open, you know,' Max said quietly.

'To see the house?' Ellie's smile was a little tight. 'Sure. Sounds like fun.'

'No.' Max had stopped eating. He was watching her face. 'The name. Marriage.'

Ellie stopped eating, too. Her appetite had vanished.

She wouldn't marry Max to give Mouse his name. Or to take it herself.

To marry Max knowing that it was in name only and that a very amicable divorce was already pencilled in?

No, thanks.

CHAPTER EIGHT

GINA the real estate agent did a double-take when she saw Ellie for the second time on the Sunday that was Mouse's two-week birthday.

Max wasn't surprised in the least. He'd been kind of stunned himself when he'd got home from work the other day after Ellie had been on her trip into town. She'd been wearing jeans that actually fitted and a soft, russet-coloured knit top that made her eyes and her hair seem the most astonishing mix of copper and chestnut shades. She'd looked…amazing and it was confusing because it wasn't so easy now to dismiss errant thoughts by reminding himself that she wasn't his 'type'.

She still didn't fit with the kind of athletic, leggy girls who were out for little more than a good time. She was different all right. Dangerously different because there was an attraction there that went a lot deeper than sex. He and Rick had always favoured blondes, too, but Ellie's hair was so *rich*. She'd said she'd only had her hair trimmed and that the hairdresser had put some rinse through it to bring out natural highlights but it *glowed* in some mysterious fashion and it looked *so* soft. His fingers had itched to bury themselves in it.

He hadn't, of course. He was being very, very careful ever since that kiss that hadn't been a kiss. Ellie valued her independence. She had some definite plans for her future that didn't include him and he didn't want to be involved. It would only complicate her life. Not to mention his. Coming to see this house was an aberration that was making him distinctly nervous for some reason. It had only been intended as an outing. There were lots of tourist attractions out here on the Otago Peninsula. Larnach Castle and the aquarium. The lighthouse and the world-famous albatross colony. It was just a bonus that he could make a foray into the world of real estate that he knew he should enter and now was probably as good a time as any.

Maybe it was because it was something he'd never done before. Or maybe it had something to do with the way Gina had been staring at Ellie as if she couldn't believe she was the same woman and Max could sympathise with the confused expression. Things were changing and Max wasn't sure about the direction they were taking. Some of it was good. He was delighted that both Ellie and Mouse had passed the assessments given in their outpatient appointments at the hospital. He could have predicted how pleased the doctors would be because he could see Ellie's strength returning day by day. She had a sparkle about her that couldn't be attributed entirely to a new wardrobe or a clever hairdresser.

Pretty soon now she'd disappear out of his life. She'd already been on the internet, checking out discount flight fares to Australia. She'd been exploring job opportunities as well and rental accommodation that might suit. The next step was to update her passport to include her child and that was only on hold until she decided on the name she wanted for her daughter.

She'd bought a book of names when she'd been in town and it had come out again last night.

'Annabelle? Bella? I quite like Bella. Oh, look… here's Maxine. It means "greatest".'

'You're not calling her Maxine.'

'She's probably going to end up being Mouse for the rest of her life,' Ellie had said mournfully. 'Mouse Peters. Doesn't have the best ring to it, does it?'

Mouse McAdam didn't sound too bad. Not that he'd pointed that out, mind you. Funny how the idea of marriage to Ellie to provide a legal name had suddenly lost its appeal. Why? Was it because he could finally see that it would be such a sham and not what any marriage should be about? Especially a marriage that involved someone like Ellie. Not that Max had ever given that much thought to the institution but, deep down, he had principles and one of them was obviously that marriage was not something that should be taken that lightly.

Who knew?

Perhaps house hunting was another aspect of grown-up life that shouldn't be taken lightly but they'd driven out along the windy peninsula road on this sunny afternoon, admiring the shards of light playing on the ruffled harbour waters. They'd had a bit of trouble locating the address, despite his satellite navigation device, because this house was set on a hillside and hidden from the road by a thick stand of native bush. Sunlight filtered through the canopy of these private woods, which effectively killed any traffic or other noise from the outside world and there was an atmosphere that made Max pause when he climbed out of the car. He had an odd feeling that he was being pushed towards something he really wasn't ready for. He gave himself a mental shake. Anyone would feel like that with a smiling real estate agent bearing down on them. He was only a potential buyer here. He could say no and he already knew he *would* say no.

The house itself was a wonderful, rambling old villa with a wisteria vine adorning the deep veranda and a view of the harbour and the green hills on the other side that would probably make it sell in a flash. They all stood for a moment at the top of the steps, their backs to the front door.

'That's Port Chalmers over there,' Max pointed out to Ellie. 'That's where Rick's place is. He's got a converted warehouse loft close to the container terminal. Very industrial. Trendy.'

'Bit different from this, then.'

'Mmm.' It was a bachelor pad all right and it hadn't had the space for the three of them when Jet had come home for a spell. Why had he offered to move somewhere else? Had he seen his new apartment as a stepping stone from bachelor pad to family home? If so, he hadn't had his feet in the interim space for nearly long enough.

'You'll love this place,' Gina said, turning to unlock the door. 'Come on. I can't wait to show you around.' She waited for them to enter the wide hallway. 'Such a cute baby,' she said as Ellie went past. 'What's his name?'

'It's a she,' Max said. 'And her name is Mouse.'

Gina giggled. 'What's her *real* name?'

There was a moment's awkward silence and then Ellie spoke. 'We haven't decided. Max doesn't like my choice so I'm waiting till he comes up with something better.'

'Fair enough.' Gina was heading for a sweeping stairway at the end of the hall. 'Let's start upstairs with the master bedroom. It's got the most amazing view.'

Max followed in silence. It was just part of the pretence, wasn't it? Ellie wasn't really expecting him to come up with a name for Mouse, was she? That was a responsibility he wasn't happy to take on but what if he didn't and she ended up calling the poor kid Maxine?

'Vacant possession,' Gina told them as they came back downstairs. 'The owner was hoping not to have to sell but he's decided to stay in

Europe and he needs the capital for his business venture.'

'It's big,' was Max's verdict as they completed the tour.

Gina nodded happily. 'Four bedrooms and the office, two bathrooms, the games room in the basement and the guest suite over the garage. It's a perfect family home.'

But he didn't have a family. Gina glanced to where Ellie was standing with Mouse in the baby sling near the French doors that opened from the open-plan kitchen living area to a terrace that flowed into a large, sloping garden. Max followed her gaze. Was Ellie admiring the backdrop of the bush or deliberately avoiding having to keep up the deception that they were just the kind of family that this house was crying out for?

'I know it might seem a bit big compared to your apartment at the moment but think of it as future-proofing,' Gina said with a smile. 'Who knows? You might end up with a few more little ones and this is the kind of house you'd want your grandchildren visiting, isn't it?'

Grandchildren? Good grief! Max saw his life telescoping inwards with him as an old man, rocking on that veranda. No, thanks. He had a hell of lot more living to do before then.

'This would be paradise for children,' Gina added, blithely unaware of the effect her comment had had. 'Tree huts in the bush. There's a little stream on the boundary and it's not much of a walk down to the harbour. You could have a boat. It's great for swimming in the summer. Or you could go fishing off the jetty.'

With the grandchildren. Ha!

Max tried to sound businesslike. 'The house is pretty old. It needs repairs as it is and would take a lot of maintenance to keep up.'

Gina smiled again. 'I'll bet you're good with a hammer and paintbrush, Max.'

'Never tried to find out.' His precious time off was put to far more enjoyable uses. Like a blast of fresh air on an open road bike ride. Or drink-

ing time with his mates. Or a hot date. Yes, he
still had a lot of living to do out there. To give up
that time to work on a house? To build tree huts
or mess about with boats? He needed to get out
of here.

He didn't have a family. He didn't even have
the prospect of one.

Carefully, Max avoided even a glance in Ellie's
direction.

'I'll think about it,' he told Gina, 'but I don't
think it's what I'm looking for at the moment.
Thanks for showing us around, though.'

'No worries. It's not on the market just yet so
you've got time to think. I'll be listing it next
week, probably.' Gina ushered them out and
locked the door behind them. 'I've got to dash.'
She winked at Max. 'I've got a date with your
friend Rick tonight.'

Max watched her slide into her little sports car
and take off with a spurt of gravel beneath the
tyres.

Dammit. *He* wanted a date with Rick. A fast

ride to nowhere. Or, rather, somewhere that had a few icy lagers on tap. He wanted to step out of this parallel universe he'd fallen into that contained big houses and tree huts and babies that needed real names and sweet-smelling, *different* women.

What the hell had happened to his life?

Max was very quiet on the way back to the apartment.

So was Ellie.

She'd seen that look on his face as Gina had driven off, having announced her upcoming date with Rick.

Max had been envious. *He* wanted to be out with Gina. Having fun. Instead, he was stuck with her. And a baby. He was probably realising just how effectively he had scuttled any chance he might have had with Gina because she believed he had a wife and child. If she hadn't already been getting the vibes during the house tour, that look on Max's face had made it very clear that the deception was past its use-by date.

Any fleeting hope that Max might even consider family life was firmly relegated to fantasyland.

Just like that perfect, perfect house with its magical setting that made it a world of its own.

Why did Mouse choose to become so grizzly as soon as they arrived home? It was almost as though she was trying to chase Max away. He certainly didn't seem inclined to hang around. A few text messages and a change of clothes and he was off.

'Going on a bike ride with Jet,' he told Ellie, when he came out of his room wearing the leather gear she hadn't seen him in since the day she'd arrived.

Sexy, sexy gear. She stood there with a howling baby in her arms and knew she didn't stand a chance with this man and she never would.

Max pulled a helmet down from above the coat

rack in the hall. 'Don't wait for me for dinner. We'll probably eat out at a pub somewhere.'

Somewhere there'd be lots of people. Attractive women who didn't have babies. There'd be music and dancing and the kind of atmosphere that was just what young doctors ordered for their time away from work.

Yes. Max couldn't wait to escape but, to his credit, he paused at the door.

'You OK being on your own for a while?'

'I'm fine. Have fun, Max.'

'Don't open the door to anyone. Text me if you get worried.'

'I'll be fine.' She could imagine what Jet's reaction would be if Max received a text from her requesting assistance. She could see that dark scowl and it was easy to imagine what he'd say to his friend.

For God's sake, man, get rid of her. She's been nothing but trouble since she got here.

It took a long time to get Mouse happy. A feed and cuddle, a bath and change of clothes. Ellie was tired by the time her daughter was asleep in her bassinette but she didn't rest herself. She got busy.

An hour later, she had printed out and filled in an application form for a job in a Melbourne hospital that boasted a nearby crèche that took babies from six weeks old upwards. She found an envelope, stuffed the form inside and then sealed it and then she closed her eyes and breathed out a sigh of relief.

She knew where she was heading.

She had a future again.

Knowing that, and knowing that her time of being close to Max McAdam was limited, there really wasn't any harm in enjoying every moment she had left.

Was there?

Something else had changed.

Max couldn't quite put his finger on what it was but maybe that night out with Jet had cleared his head. Which was weird, seeing as he'd ended up leaving his bike at a mate's house, getting a taxi home in the early hours of the morning and waking up with a mother of a hangover.

Ellie had been very considerate the next day, keeping well out of his way with a shopping trip that resulted in a pushchair that she then took Mouse for a long walk in. He'd barely noticed them and it wasn't until several days later that he realised he still wasn't noticing them.

No, that wasn't quite right. He knew they were there well enough but it wasn't creating any negative-type tension. Yes, that was what it was. For whatever reason, after he'd burned off the fear of ending up rocking on a veranda having had his entire life sucked away, a new serenity had slipped into his life.

Max came to this satisfactory conclusion as he watched over Mouse while Ellie had a shower and washed her hair late one evening. Mouse was awake and he'd picked her up but she didn't seem to be uncomfortable or hungry so he was sitting on the couch with the baby lying on his lap, the back of her head resting on his knees. She was gripping his forefingers with those miniature fists and looking up at him with an amusingly serious expression.

'How's it going?' Max asked. 'I've had a good day. How 'bout you?'

It had been a good day. A good week, actually, with a huge variety of interesting cases. Having someone to come home to who was genuinely interested in hearing about everything he'd been doing was the best way to debrief he'd ever come across. Living with Rick and Jet, the last thing any of them felt inclined to do out of hours was rehash a working day but Ellie seemed to revel in it. She could ask the kind of questions that made him realise what a good job he'd done or sometimes make him think about how he could do it even better next time. And sometimes, best of all, he could make her laugh.

Like he had tonight.

'So this guy comes in like the hounds of hell are chasing him. He's as white as a sheet.

Bloodstained tea-towel wrapped around one hand and a bag of frozen veggies in the other. Tells us he's chopped his finger off and it's in with the frozen peas and then he faints into a puddle on the floor.'

'Oh, no! What did you do?'

'Cleared Trauma One. Put out a call to Neurosurgery and Rick happens to be in the department for something else so he gets all excited about the possibility of reattaching a finger and then...'

'What?'

'We unwrap the tea-towel and find he's only nicked the very top off his finger. Flesh wound. All he needed was a sticky plaster.'

And Ellie had laughed. A wonderful ripple of sound that made Max feel proud of his ability to entertain. Made him feel...important, somehow. Made him feel really good, anyway.

'I miss it,' Ellie had confessed. 'Maybe it's just as well I can't afford to be a full-time mum for too long. It'll be good to get back to work and you know what?'

'What?'

'I think I'll go into Emergency this time instead of going back to Theatre work.'

'Join the Band-Aid brigade?'

'The reason that's so funny is because it's so far towards the other end of the spectrum for the kind of life-and-death stuff you deal with every day. The variety is amazing. Challenging. I can see why you love it so much.'

And Max could see why Ellie might want to be a full-time mother for as long as she could afford to.

He was watching a play of facial movements in the tiny features in his lap. A furrowed brow that made the mouse look cross and then a wrinkled nose as if she'd smelt something particularly offensive. The tiny cupid's bow of a mouth was open and the tip of a pink tongue emerged and then disappeared again.

Max found himself poking the tip of his own

tongue out to mirror the action. Mouse's eyes widened. Max widened his own eyes. And then he found himself sitting there, holding the hands of a three-week-old baby, making the most ridiculous faces he could.

Mouse seemed to love it. He could swear she was trying to copy him. She definitely followed a tongue-poking manoeuvre. It was fascinating. Just as rewarding as making Ellie laugh. He was making sounds without realising what he was doing for a while. Clicking his tongue and talking—God help him—in baby talk. And then it happened. The corners of that little mouth stretched and curled.

Mouse smiled at him.

Ellie didn't believe him when she came back. She sat on the end of the couch, combing out her hair, and paused to shake her head.

'She's too young to smile. They're not supposed to do that until they're about six weeks old.'

'She did. She smiled at me. Didn't you?' Max

lifted the tiny hands and clicked his tongue again, trying to elicit a repeat of the miracle smile.

'Maybe she had wind.'

'Nope. It was a smile. Look…*look*…she's doing it again.'

Sure enough, she was, even if it was just with one side of her mouth this time.

'Oh, my God,' Ellie breathed. 'She *is* smiling.'

They both stared at Mouse. And then they looked up to stare at each other and after a long, long moment, they both smiled.

Max had to look away. He needed to move, in fact. Handing Ellie her baby, he stood up. He walked aimlessly across the room towards the bookshelf where his gaze fell on the 'bad boys' photograph. The four of them.

Slowly, he turned back to Ellie.

'What about Mattie?' he asked quietly.

'Your friend?'

'No. The name.'

She got it. She looked down at Mouse and then

back up at him and she still looked like she had after seeing her baby smile for the first time.

'Short for Matilda,' she whispered. 'Mattie. It's perfect, Max, but are you sure?'

'Sounds good to me.'

'But I'd be naming her after someone that was very special to you.'

It was kind of difficult to swallow. 'It's what I'd choose for her name,' he said gruffly. 'If she was mine.'

Ellie's gaze slid away and she seemed to be blinking fast. 'Matilda it is, then.' She leaned down to kiss her baby. 'Hello, Mattie.'

He had given Mouse her real name.

The name he would have chosen for his own child.

The joy of what was a priceless gift was still with Ellie when she had tucked a very sleepy baby into the bassinette in the room they shared. She had a dreamy smile playing on her lips when she went back to the living area to find Max turning out all the lights. She could see him illuminated only by the soft glow coming from the hallway behind her.

'I thought you'd gone to bed,' he said.

'I wanted to say thank you.'

'Hey…no worries.'

If he hadn't smiled at her she could have just said something else and turned away but that smile… So real. So heartbreakingly tender. It was enough to undo her utterly. Ellie stepped forward, closing the gap between them, standing on tiptoe as she reached up to hug Max. Instinct told her she could communicate how much that gift meant—how much his friendship meant—far better through touch than words that could only be inadequate.

His arms went around her and pulled her closer. His head was bent over hers and she heard the deliberate, indrawn breath—as though Max was revelling in the scent of her hair. Of *her*.

She could feel his body against hers. The solid wall of his chest on her breasts. The imprint of every finger against her back. A pressure on her belly that brought a shaft of desire so intense she had to close her eyes tightly and try—desperately—to remember why it was she couldn't let Max know how she really felt about him.

Maybe she wasn't succeeding very well. When the hug finally loosened—way after it should have, given a status of friendly gratitude—and Ellie cracked her eyes open, she found Max watching her and she could see what appeared to be a reflection of exactly how *she* was feeling in the dark depths of his eyes.

'Ellie…'

Her name was a whisper. A half-groan. A warning perhaps. Or a question.

She didn't respond. Not verbally, anyway. Instead, she allowed her body to overrule any conscious thought. She kept her arms around Max's neck, went back on tiptoe and tilted her head, parting her lips.

Offering him her mouth.

Her body.

The sound Max made was most definitely a groan this time. His mouth covered hers and it was no casual brush. His lips found the shape of her mouth, locked onto it and then took it on a journey like none Ellie had ever experienced. A roller-coaster of movement. Pressure that built and then fell away into shards of sensation she could feel way down low in her belly. The most delicious sliding of his tongue teasing hers as his hands cradled her head, his fingers buried deep in her hair.

Finally, she could do what she'd been itching to do for so long and feel the roughness of that shadowed jaw under her fingers and then her palms as she slid her hands up to loosen the waves of his hair and glory in the silky slide as she explored the shape of his whole head.

And then his lips dropped away from hers to touch the side of her neck and Ellie tipped her head back to offer him her throat.

Her life.

'Ellie…' This time her name was a growl of frustration. 'We can't do this.'

Ellie froze. She couldn't ask why not. She couldn't even *think* why not.

'It's too soon.'

The statement was bewildering. How could it be too soon when she felt like this? So totally in love with him. But she couldn't tell him that because then he would run and this would *never* happen. She'd be gone soon and she'd never know what it could have been like, except in her fantasies.

'You only gave birth a few weeks ago. If we don't stop this, I won't—'

'I'm fine,' Ellie interrupted. She held the eye contact without wavering. 'I'm fine,' she repeated in a whisper. 'I didn't need stitches. I—' Oh, God… What could she say that wouldn't sound like begging? If he wanted to stop, she had to respect that. 'I'm fine,' she repeated simply, her voice trailing into silence.

I want this, she tried to tell him with her eyes. *As long as you want it too.*

Max must have picked up at least something of her unspoken message. He closed his eyes for a heartbeat and then he picked Ellie up. Swept her into his arms effortlessly and carried her into his room.

Into his bed.

Their next kiss took them to a whole new level and with it came the shedding of clothes and the touch of skin on skin. A new roller-coaster that was as much of an emotional as a physical ride.

Ellie offered Max her heart.

Her soul.

You could give someone a name and still keep it.

You could give someone your heart when it was still right there inside you, keeping you alive.

Such gifts were treasures that were the most precious things you could own and nobody could take them away from you.

Ellie was musing on the wonder of it all as she took Mouse…no, Mattie…for a ride in her push-chair late the following afternoon.

She was walking slowly, a little weary after her amazing night, but she'd never been this happy.

Ever.

Not even when she'd seen her baby for the first time or felt her suckling at her breast. Or when she'd felt the first stirrings of her love for Max in that moment of connection when he'd been there to witness her feeding Mattie for the first time. And when he'd chosen a name that meant so much to him and offered it to her daughter. Or even when she'd held him in her arms last night when he'd come apart and cried out her name in the wake of her own astonishing climax.

No. This feeling was bigger. A combination of all of those things and it encompassed all the people involved. Herself. Max. Mattie.

Even if it only lasted a matter of days. Even if Max had no idea he was such an integral part of it, *this* was what family felt like. Separate beings welded together by love. By the gifts that you could give and still keep.

She and Mattie were only going as far as the

corner shop. Ellie was cooking dinner for Max and wanted it to be very special. She'd been to the supermarket earlier and thought she had everything, right down to the bottle of champagne chilling in the fridge.

Max didn't have to know what she was really celebrating. She intended to tell him it was a name-warming for Mattie. And then she thought it could be her one-month birthday but that needed a cake and when she went to start baking one, she discovered they had run out of butter. No big deal. It was a short walk to the shop and, now that she thought about it, there was a postbox there as well. She could buy the butter *and* finally post that application form. Silly to keep putting it off when it might mean she missed out on the opportunity altogether.

The walk took her past the motel where she'd spent her first day away from the hospital. The place she'd never gone back to, not wanting to claim the old clothes that were part of a life she intended leaving well behind. The memories of her brief stay there were decidedly unpleasant. Echoes of the abuse being shouted still hung in the air. If she looked down the driveway as she walked past she'd be able to see the spot where Nigel had landed in front of her unit. Had the bloodstains been cleaned away?

Not that she really wanted to know but it was inevitable that her head turned in that direction as she reached the motel's entranceway. What she saw made her stop in her tracks. Blink hard and look again because she couldn't believe what she *was* seeing.

Right there—in the exact spot Nigel had been sprawled after his fall from the balcony above— lay another shape. A small one.

A *child?*

Ellie could feel the blood draining from her head. A curious buzzing sound filled her ears, which probably explained why she hadn't heard the woman crying out for help. A woman who was now running towards her.

Was this one of Nigel's children? Had they been

climbing on the balcony? Had it been damaged by the accident and never repaired? She hadn't taken much notice of his wife that night. It could be her rushing down the driveway.

'*Help,*' the woman begged. She grabbed Ellie's arm. 'Please…he's fallen. Can you help?'

'Of course.' Ellie jerked the pushchair to turn it but the wheels were locked somehow and it almost tipped.

'I'll take care of her,' the woman gasped. 'Please…I don't know what to do. I don't know if he's breathing…'

Ellie ran to the child, pulling her phone from her pocket. She'd just check the boy's airway and then call for an ambulance. She knelt down and tipped the child's head back carefully. His eyes snapped open and he grinned up at her.

'Do I get my ten dollars now?'

'*What?*'

Ellie's heart was pounding painfully and her head was still buzzing. What kind of *stupid* prank was this? He'd scared her half to death.

Had scared his mother. She flicked her head sideways, opening her mouth to call out. To reassure the woman that this child was fine and there'd been no need to panic.

And that was when her heart stopped.

Because the woman was nowhere to be seen.

And neither was the pushchair containing her own child.

CHAPTER NINE

OF ALL the events that had occurred to turn his life upside down in the last month, this was by far the worst.

It was an unimaginable horror.

Max had received the call at work just as he'd been due to finish his shift. He'd been having a coffee with Jet and Rick, in fact, and the other two men had stiffened to attention as they'd heard his stunned silence and the staccato questions of a man intent on gaining control of an unacceptable situation.

'What's happened?

'What's being done?

'Where *is* she right now?'

They had all ridden their bikes to work that day. They might have arrived at different times but they left as a single unit. Three powerful machines with black-clad men hunched over them as they sped towards the same destination.

The motel where the police had been talking to Ellie.

She looked like a ghost. A small, terrified wraith.

If Rick and Jet were surprised by the way Max strode into the motel manager's office, pushing through the throng of uniformed police officers to gather Ellie into his arms, they did no more than exchange a loaded glance.

Every occupant of the room watched the embrace that followed. The way Ellie clung to Max as though her life depended on it. The way the tall, leather-clad man curled his body so protectively over hers.

The bond was unmistakable.

So powerful that Rick sent another glance at the man standing at his shoulder. Jet merely quirked an eyebrow and then nodded, albeit with resignation. The significance had been noted. The importance of this mission had just been upgraded to a red alert.

'You're Dr Max McAdam?' A senior police officer had apparently decided enough was enough when it came to a comforting embrace.

'Yes,' Max growled.

'And you've been posing as Ms Peters's husband? The father of this missing child?'

'He told *me* he was her brother.' The motel manager looked up from where another officer was taking his statement.

Max took a deep breath. He moved so that he could face the senior officer but he didn't let go of Ellie. He tucked her against his side with an arm that enclosed her completely.

'That's correct.' He held the gaze of the man speaking to him. He was more than prepared to defend his actions and if anyone threatened this woman he held, they'd better be prepared for a battle. 'And you are?'

'Detective Inspector Jack Davidson.' The officer was taking Max's measure. 'Jack,' he added, his tone suggesting that he was impressed by what he was seeing. His gaze slid to Ellie. 'We've been told about the behaviour of Dr Marcus Jones. I believe you were a witness to his pursuit of this young woman? Following her to Dunedin?'

'Also correct.'

'The man's a weasel.' Rick's drawl floated across the room.

Jack Davidson ignored the interjection. 'You're also aware that he's the real father of Ms Peters's baby?'

Max scowled. No, he wanted to say. The real father would have been there to do the kangaroo care his baby had needed at birth.

He would have been the one to witness the miracle of that first breastfeeding.

He would have seen that first smile.

He would have cherished Ellie, dammit. Realised what an amazing woman she was and won her trust so that he could have experienced the joy of making love to her, not forcing her because he'd decided that was what *he* wanted.

Max could feel his blood beginning to boil. A real father wouldn't have separated his baby from her mother. He would have moved heaven and earth to keep them together. To keep them safe. The way he had every intention of doing, so help him.

'Dr McAdam? Max?' The tone was impatient.

'Biologically, yes,' Max snapped.

But Mouse's *real* father?

He was that person. And he always would be as far as he was concerned. Would it make any difference to Ellie if she knew how he felt? That he loved her child and would protect her with his life, if necessary? He gave her the softest squeeze to try and convey that he was there. Heart and soul.

'We've confirmed that it was Marcus Jones who visited Mr Grimsby, the manager here, yesterday and obtained all the details he could regarding Ms Peters's stay here and the incident that prompted her departure.'

'He said he was a lawyer,' the manager protested. 'That Miss Peters was planning to sue. That he could get a court order if I didn't co-operate and that he could make sure my business got wrecked.'

Max ignored the interruption. 'I still don't understand how this happened. How he managed to take Mouse.'

'Mouse?' The detective inspector frowned. 'You mean—?'

'It was my fault,' Ellie said quietly. Her voice was oddly calm. Expressionless. 'I left her. I practically handed her over. I—'

'This *wasn't* your fault,' Max told her firmly. He could be perfectly sure about that without knowing any of the details.

'Ellie was taken in by what appears to be a carefully set-up ruse,' Jack Davidson told Max. 'We're currently trying to track the woman involved who offered to look after the baby while Ellie went to the aid of a child who seemed to have fallen from an upstairs balcony here.'

Max tightened his hold on Ellie. The *bastard*. He must have heard the details of the accident and known exactly what kind of buttons it would push for someone who had the training to help. Especially using a child. There was no way Ellie wouldn't have been sucked in. He would have been himself.

But she pulled away from his touch. She wrapped her own arms around herself and looked as though she was staring at something a million miles away.

'It was *my* fault,' she whispered.

'We've got a good description of the woman from several people and—' The detective broke off as the radio clipped to his shoulder crackled into life. He answered with a call sign.

'Jack?' Everybody could hear the voice on the other end. 'We've located the pushchair.'

Ellie gasped but everybody else seemed to be holding their breath.

'Any sign of the baby?' the detective snapped. A moment's silence and then came the response. 'No.'

How could one of the smallest words in existence create such agony?

Ellie couldn't move. She couldn't speak. She couldn't even cry. The atmosphere in the room was changing. People were moving and things were happening but she couldn't focus on what was being said. This was a nightmare and she had no control over any of it.

After a bewildering length of time, she found herself being led out of the motel office.

'Keep her in your apartment, then,' she heard someone say reluctantly. 'Don't go anywhere.'

'If any contact whatsoever is made,' another voice ordered, 'let us know. Immediately. We'll keep you informed of any developments on our side.'

Max walked her to his apartment. He tried to put his arm around her again but Ellie couldn't bear it. She had to hold onto herself because her heart was ripped open and this was the only way to hold the pieces together. If she let go—relaxed even the tiniest bit—she might actually die.

When she entered the apartment and saw the table that she'd set for the special dinner she'd planned for Max it all morphed together into the same, ghastly nightmare.

If she hadn't fallen in love she wouldn't have set the table like that. With candles and glasses ready to fill with champagne. She wouldn't have thought of baking a cake and wouldn't have gone on that fateful walk to the shop.

She wouldn't have lost her baby.

'He won't hurt her,' Max said gently. Did he want to believe that because the alternative was simply unthinkable?

Ellie spun around. '*You* don't know that.' She knew more than he did. The fear lying like a dead weight inside her was growing. Starting to send tendrils right into her veins.

'I know it's you that he wants.' Max raised his

hands as though he wanted to touch Ellie. She took a step backwards. She couldn't cope with being comforted. Didn't *deserve* to be. Max dropped his hands by his sides. 'He's using Mouse as bait. He can't afford to hurt her.'

Why not? How would she know what he was doing? Maybe he was just doing this to punish her.

'He'll call,' Max said. 'And then we'll know where he is and the police can get him. They'll find Mouse and bring her back safely.'

She was Mouse again. Not Mattie.

Why? Because she was so tiny and defenceless? Or because the person she'd been named for had died a dreadful, and possibly unnecessary, death?

Ellie squeezed herself more tightly to try and hold back the wave of pain. She tried to shake the black thoughts away. The effort was so great that her breath escaped in an agonised sob and her legs felt so much like jelly she had to let herself sink onto the couch. She pulled her legs up beneath her, curling into the corner. She could hear the rumble of motorbikes outside. She could even feel it, against her skin.

No…that was her phone vibrating. Oh…*God…* was this it? *Contact?*

She fumbled for her phone as Max was moving to open the front door. Rick came in.

'Jet's gone back to get your bike,' he told Max.

Ellie had managed to open her phone to find a text message.

Don't talk to anyone, it said. *Or you won't see her again.*

She snapped the phone shut as Max turned but he hadn't missed the action.

'You got a message?' There was an urgency in his voice that she'd never heard before. Pain, even.

Every instinct Ellie had was to tell Max. To show him the message. To share the horror and have these men help to make a plan and deal with it. They would protect her and Mouse. The dark angels.

But, if she did, Marcus might know somehow and he might hurt her baby. He was capable of it, she knew that better than anyone. He'd hurt *her*, hadn't he?

'N-no,' Ellie stammered. 'I was just…hoping.'

Max held her gaze with a look that broke her heart all over again. He understood. He was feeling this, too. Then he gave a single, curt nod.

'He would have got the landline number from the motel records. He'll probably ring here.'

The phone in the apartment did ring a short time later, after Jet had joined the tense group. Ellie uncurled her legs, ready to jump from the couch, but Max got to the phone first.

'They've traced the woman and arrested her,' he reported after what seemed an interminably long conversation. 'She was paid to set it all up and snatch Mouse. She handed her over to Marcus at the corner shop as arranged. He abandoned the pushchair and took off in a vehicle. One that he rented at the airport and apparently requested a baby seat for. The police have the details. They've got all the manpower they have available searching now.'

Ellie could feel her phone vibrating silently in her pocket again.

'They've got the airport covered,' Max continued. 'And they're watching the main roads in and out of the city.'

Ellie managed to nod. Then she stood up. Three men stilled. Three sets of dark eyes were fixed on her.

'I…um…need to go to the loo,' she said.

In the privacy of the bathroom, she opened her phone with trembling fingers. The text message this time was an address. A road she'd never heard of.

Come alone, the message finished. *Or else.*

Ellie splashed cold water on her face, trying to rinse away the nausea that made her stomach roil. She had to try and think. What the hell was she going to do now?

Tell Max.

No. If she did, he would go instead of her. Probably without taking the risk of including the police. These guys didn't always follow the rules, did they? Not when someone's life was at stake and they might be able to do something themselves. And if he went instead of her, Marcus would hurt Max. And if he hurt Max, what would stop him from hurting Mouse? To punish her for sending someone else. For disobeying him.

She stood to lose the two people she loved most in the entire world.

But if she went herself, there was a chance she could sort this out. What if she could persuade Marcus that she'd made a mistake? That she wanted to be with him and their child? He couldn't keep her isolated completely and she could use the first opportunity she had to call for help.

To call the police.

And Max.

Yes. The more she thought about it, the more the idea seemed the best choice she had. Maybe the only choice because the safety of her baby had to be her first consideration and what did she have to go on?

The knowledge that Marcus had Mouse.

The fact that he wanted *her*.

All she had to do was convince him that he'd won for long enough to save Mouse.

And then what?

Would Max still want to have anything to do with her given the amount of trouble she'd caused? There was a new pain to be found going down that track so it was just as well she couldn't afford to think that far ahead. She couldn't handle thinking of anything more than how to get where she needed to be. To where Marcus was. And Mouse.

The ache in her breasts went up several notches to become unbearable. They were heavy with the milk that Mouse must be getting desperate for by now. Marcus might have requested a baby seat in the rental vehicle but had he thought to provide a bottle? Or nappies? Highly unlikely.

Another reason why she had to be the one to go. And surely Max would be grateful that she hadn't made things worse for him and his friends?

But how could she get out of there without giving herself away?

How could she find where this address was?

How could she get there?

Think, she ordered herself. Take a deep breath and think. *There has to be a way.*

A minute later, with shaking fingers, she managed to send a return message.

I'm on my way.

Something had happened in those couple of minutes that Ellie had been in the bathroom, Max decided.

She'd gone in there looking as though she couldn't string two coherent thoughts together and she had come out looking...focused.

Weirdly calm.

He went into the kitchen to make coffee. Ellie sat on the couch. Rick and Jet sat at the table which had place settings for two, he noted belatedly. And, good grief...candles?

Had Ellie been planning a romantic dinner

tonight? Food, in various stages of preparation, was scattered over the bench top. A fresh-looking salad. Mushrooms, sliced and ready to sauté. Was there steak in the fridge? And, if so, how had Ellie known what his all-time favourite dinner was? Not that he was remotely hungry right now. And a romantic dinner seemed like a bad-taste joke.

Had it only been last night that they had stepped over the boundaries of friendship and into the realm of lovers?

It didn't seem real. Maybe Ellie was regretting it and that was why she didn't want him touching her any more. Perhaps she considered him some kind of distraction now and if she hadn't been distracted she wouldn't have become separated from Mouse.

Mattie.

Oh…God. Silently, Max placed mugs of coffee in front of Rick and Jet. What would they think if they knew he'd given their missing mate's name to the baby who was now also missing?

Rick would probably shake his head sadly.

Jet would give him a look that would tell him he'd been crazy getting into any of this in the first place.

Max went back into the kitchen for the other two mugs. He walked towards Ellie, trying to decide if she'd want him to sit on the couch with her or join the others at the table, leaving her separate. Alone.

He couldn't do that. Max sat on the couch beside her. She was still hugging herself and he noticed the way her hands were shaking.

'You cold?'

'Mmm.'

'Drink this. It'll help warm you up.'

But Ellie shook her head, declining the coffee. 'No, thanks...I think I might have a shower.'

'Good idea.' Odd, but maybe it would distract her from this awful waiting as well as warming her up. He wasn't surprised Ellie was feeling cold. Dread was sitting in his own gut like a block of ice.

'Will you call me if...if someone rings?'

'Of course.' Max watched helplessly as Ellie went into the hallway, closing the door behind her. Leave it open, he wanted to call, but why would she want to when the house was full of men?

With a heavy sigh, Max got to his feet again. He took the unwanted coffee into the kitchen and tipped it down the sink. Then he took the other mug and joined his friends at the table.

The conversation was spasmodic.

'Maybe he won't call,' Jet suggested. 'Maybe it's the kid he wants.'

Rick shook his head. 'Nah. Didn't you *see* the way he looked at Ellie that day? Hear the way he spoke to her? The creep thinks he owns her.'

'He doesn't give a damn about the baby,' Max said through gritted teeth. 'Or he wouldn't have taken her away from her mother.'

'He'll call.' Rick sounded confident. 'And I intend to be there when they corner the bastard.'

'We're not doing anything that could put Mouse in any danger,' Max said fiercely. 'No way.'

* * *

The phone rang again and Max activated the speaker.

'Max?'

'Yeah.'

'Jack Davidson. There's been a possible sighting of the vehicle Jones hired but…' The detective sounded puzzled. 'It's way out on the peninsula. Does that make any kind of sense to you?'

'No.' It didn't. It was a dead-end road. Miles away from any kind of escape from the city unless it was to be by boat and even Marcus Jones couldn't be that crazy, could he? 'Ellie's never even… Oh, wait…we did take a drive out there recently to look at a house that was for sale.'

Jet's eyebrows rose eloquently.

'They were just looking,' Rick told Jet in a stage whisper. 'Gina told me all about it.'

'We'll follow the lead up,' the detective finished. 'Any contact been made at your end?'

'No.'

After the call, silence fell amongst the three men. Jet got up and paced the living area.

'Bit poky in here, isn't it?'

'I've gone off the whole area,' Max admitted. 'And I'm going to have to move soon in any case. Sarah sent me an email to say she's coming back.'

'Who? Oh, the chick who sub-leased you this place?' Jet paused to stare out the window. 'Wasn't she going to the States to find the father of her sick kid?'

'Turned out he wasn't the father after a DNA test.'

'Bummer.'

'Yeah. He put Sarah onto another possibility, though. Josh's mother had just broken up with another guy when he met her. He was also a doctor who worked at Auckland Central. Thinks his name is Richard someone. Or someone Richard.'

'How old is the kid?' Jet was pacing again.

'Dunno.' Max had only one child on his mind right now. 'Around seven or eight, I guess.'

Jet's teeth gleamed as he grinned at Rick. 'Guess that lets you off the hook, mate.'

'Get off the grass. I'm careful about stuff like that.'

Another silence fell. Maybe they were all thinking about a time a little further back in their lives. Ten years ago, when they'd all dealt with their grief over Matt in different ways. Jet had taken up martial arts. Max had taken on some intensive postgraduate studies. Rick had been drinking a lot. And partying. Hard. Being careful might not have been high on his agenda for a while there so it was just as well the time-frame wasn't compatible.

Max's thoughts drifted back to what was threatening to overwhelm him but did he want to start a conversation about Marcus Jones and what he might be capable of doing to a baby?

What he might do to Ellie if he ever got close enough to her again.

It wasn't the first time a kind of telepathy had occurred between these men.

'She's taking a hell of a long time in that shower, isn't she?'

'Yeah…' Max shoved his chair back. 'I might go and check on her.'

He could hear the shower running as he stepped into the narrow hallway but he got no response when he knocked on the bathroom door.

'Ellie? You OK?' He opened the door to a wall of steam.

For a moment, it was hard to see anything in the small room but when Max stepped in, he could see quite well enough through the condensation on the glass walls of the shower.

The water was running but there was nobody standing beneath it and in that split second of realisation Max knew there never had been.

With an oath, he shut off the water. Three long steps was all it took to get him back to the door of the living room.

'She's gone,' he said, his tone as hollow as his gut.

'*What?* Where?'

'To meet the weasel, of course,' Jet said impatiently. 'How does she know where to go?'

'Her phone.' Max breathed out another soft curse. 'I *thought* she'd got a message but she denied it.'

'She was probably following instructions.'

'But how can she go anywhere? Unless it's on foot?'

Max took a swift glance at the hook beside the coat rack. 'My car keys are gone.'

He moved towards the phone. 'I'd better call Davidson.'

'Wait.' Jet wasn't pacing any longer. He was standing very still. 'We know where she's going.'

'Yeah…to meet some deranged bastard who's got her baby.'

Jet shook his head impatiently. 'His vehicle's been sighted on the peninsula road, yes?'

Max and Rick stared at him.

'How hard could it be to catch up with an SUV on that road?'

An exchange of glances was all it took.

The three men reached for their helmets.

Seconds later and they were outside the apartment, kicking their bikes into life.

With a roar of intent, they sped off into the night.

CHAPTER TEN

VALUABLE time had been lost while Ellie tried to remember how to programme the satellite navigation device in Max's car but now she was well on her way.

But where on earth was she going?

It seemed to be the route she and Max had taken the day they'd gone to view that house. Along Andersons Bay Road. Onto Portobello Road with the dark expanse of the harbour on her left. But why would Marcus want to come way out here?

Because it was isolated?

Was he planning to *kill* her?

No. While the thought was terrifying, Ellie didn't believe it. Marcus Jones was a respected surgeon. His reputation and career meant everything to him. He was obsessive, yes, and very, very angry that she was refusing to do what he wanted her to do, but murder? Unthinkable. And even if she was in danger—and she knew perfectly well that she was being stupid going off on her own like this—what mattered was the safety of her child. If she lost her own life in saving Mattie, so be it. The drive to protect her baby was strong enough to override everything else.

She couldn't go as fast as she wanted on this road because of its twists and turns but she was keeping ahead of any other traffic. The frequent glances into the rear-view mirror, fearing the flashing lights of an overtaking police vehicle, showed nothing very close at all. There were lights behind her but they were going at much the same speed she was and they disappeared for a while each time she took a bend. Nothing to worry about.

Max would have found the shower running without her by now and Ellie felt a twist of remorse at deceiving him. He didn't deserve that. But he did deserve her protection and keeping him well away from Marcus Jones was the best thing she could do as far as not causing him any further trouble. He wouldn't have hesitated to jump in boots and all. That was one of the things she loved most about him. His strong sense of right and wrong and the absolute need to help someone in trouble. He'd be frustrated right now because he wouldn't have any idea of where she was going. She didn't even know herself. Even if he'd told the police she was missing they would have no clue as to where to begin looking either.

The image of Max, on the phone maybe, rubbing his forehead and frowning with concern... for *her*...sent a wave of longing through Ellie. A desire to reassure him. A desperate need to feel his arms around her.

She gripped the steering-wheel so tightly her fingers started losing sensation. She had to concentrate. She had bought some time but would it be enough? Marcus was hardly a patient man and this journey seemed to be going on for ever. She had gone past Portobello and onto Harrington Point Road from where they had turned up the hill to that house. The fleeting thought that Marcus had somehow known how much she loved the property and had purchased it as some kind of bribe could be dismissed because this was obviously nowhere near the end of this road where she'd been ordered to go.

She lost sight of the harbour. The countryside her headlights picked out was barren. Dry, rocky grass-covered hills with patches of gorse but little else. The harbour might be invisible but there was a new vast darkness on her right. The open sea, well below some dramatic-looking cliffs. No flashing lights behind her, though she did catch a glimpse around one corner of a vehicle's lights. Maybe two cars were following because there seemed to be more than two lights. Who would be travelling this road at night? A farmer? The person who looked after the lighthouse? Wildlife officers who had work to do at the albatross colony maybe? That thought was comforting. It would be nice to think there was someone else not too far away when she reached her destination.

Finally, she got to where Harrington Point Road ended. In a car park for people who wanted to visit the tourist attraction of the albatross colony. A cluster of buildings had security lights on but there were no signs of any activity so the only other car in this area had to belong to the person who had brought her there. It was too dark to see if it was occupied but then came a flash of light. And another. The bright, white glare of an automated lighthouse signal.

Ellie could see the other car was empty. Of adults, at least, but was Mouse in there? She killed the engine of Max's car and fumbled for her safety belt, her feet hitting the ground at a run the instant she'd climbed out. Her path took her straight to the other vehicle, to peer in through the windows in the desperate hope of seeing an occupied baby seat but the interior was empty and in that moment of utter desolation Ellie felt the buzz of the phone in her pocket.

Walk towards the lighthouse, the message read. *You'll see where I am.*

The gust of wind Ellie stepped into was cold but nothing on the ice that was running in her veins as she followed the new instruction. She stumbled on the rough roadway because, in between the flashes of the lighthouse beacon, it was so dark. On and on she went. She could see the lighthouse clearly with its white walls and the darker dome of its tip but she couldn't see anyone standing nearby.

With each brief illumination, she turned her head further, frantically searching for the man who was waiting for her. He wasn't close to the lighthouse at all. He had gone past signs warning of the danger of the nearby cliffs and he was standing very close to where the land beneath his feet appeared to vanish.

Ellie was much closer when the next flash of light came. She saw that Marcus was holding the handle of a baby's car seat in one hand.

And he was smiling.

* * *

They had to kill the engines of the bikes as soon as they saw the vehicle Ellie was driving pull to a stop but they could coast some distance down the hill in silence. They had already switched off their headlamps before rounding the last bend in the road.

'We'll go the rest of the way on foot,' Jet told his companions. 'How fit are you guys feeling?'

'Fit enough,' came Max's terse response. 'Let's go.'

'Got a phone call to make first,' Jet said calmly. 'Not a good look to have the back-up arriving too far past the action.'

Abandoning the bikes, the three men travelled fast on foot but they were still well behind Ellie when she got close to the lighthouse. They paused as they saw her turn off the pathway.

'Where the hell is she going? There's nothing but cliffs over there.'

'*He's* there,' Max hissed. 'Wait for the light. See?'

They saw. The lone figure and the small shape of the car seat.

Ellie a matter of metres away.

Open ground around them. No chance to get behind Marcus and take him down and if he saw any of them approaching, he could drop that car seat—and Mouse—over the cliffs beside him.

If Ellie got close enough, she could meet the same fate.

And there was nothing at all Max could do about it.

He'd never felt so helpless in his life. There was fury, there, too. At Ellie, for putting herself in danger like this. What the hell was he going to do if something happened to her? His life wouldn't be worth living.

Why?

Because he *loved* her, dammit. He loved Ellie and he loved Mouse and it didn't matter that they had turned his life upside down. He wanted it to stay that way. He didn't want to lose either of them. He *couldn't…*

Don't move, Ellie, he prayed silently. *Don't get any closer. Wait…*

'The lighthouse,' Jet said softly. 'It's as close as we can get and it'll give us cover. Wait for the light to go past and then run like hell.'

'Marcus?' Ellie stopped. Instinct was telling her not to get close enough to be touched. Not yet, anyway. Not unless she had no other choice. 'What are you doing?'

'Waiting for you, Eleanor.'

She closed her eyes for a heartbeat. How was she going to play this? Would he want her to seem weak and helpless? But hadn't she just demonstrated she wasn't by getting here at all? There was only one thing she wanted to say right now.

'I want my baby.' She swallowed hard. 'Please… give her back to me.'

'*My* baby, too, Eleanor. *Isn't* she?'

No, Ellie wanted to scream. She's mine. And… and Max's. He gave her the name of his special friend. The name he would have chosen for his own child.

'*Isn't* she?' The snarl was almost a shriek.

'Y-yes. Yes, she is.'

'No lies this time. You haven't got your let's-pretend-we're-tough-guy-bikie doctor friends around to help you this time, have you?'

'No.' Oh, dear Lord…she wished she did. All three of them. In their black leather gear. Tall and menacing and ready to protect her. But she didn't have her dark angels. She had to protect herself. And her baby.

'I'm sorry, Marcus,' she said shakily. 'I didn't mean to lie to you.'

'Yes, you did. You're lying now, you stupid cow.'

'I…I was scared. I'm still scared…' No problem sounding genuine now. *'Please,* Marcus. I'll do anything you want. Just…don't hurt her.'

The icy wind was gusting. Biting through her clothing. Was Mouse freezing? Ellie could hear a thin whimper of sound but it was unlike any noise she'd ever heard from her baby before. It sounded…exhausted. Alarming.

'She's cold, Marcus,' Ellie said desperately. 'And hungry. I need to feed her. Please…'

'Come and get her, then.'

She couldn't do that. She had to get Marcus away from the edge of the cliff but she couldn't think of any way to achieve that. Paralysed by fear, Ellie simply stood there. Waiting for another flash of light. Listening to… What was that?

Marcus heard something too. 'What the *hell* is that?' he yelled. 'You told someone where you were going, didn't you?'

'No. I promise. I didn't tell anyone.'

The noise was getting louder. She looked over her shoulder and up at the sky. The tiny flashing lights of an aircraft were clearly visible and the sound was taking on the recognisable 'chop' of helicopter rotors. Was help coming? Did she simply need to find some way of stalling Marcus? Distracting him, maybe?

'We need to go somewhere they won't be able to see us, Marcus. We have to hide. Quickly!'

'What? No…I—'

'It's all right. Listen, we'll get away from here. I'll tell the police it was all a mistake. That you didn't kidnap anybody. That we're together. You know, engaged…' She turned towards the lighthouse. 'Come with me.'

The helicopter had activated a powerful searchlight. An area that included the car park was being looked at while it hovered overhead.

'You don't want me,' Marcus sneered. 'You want *him*. You think I don't know what you've been doing? Playing happy families. Going to look at houses to buy?'

'No. It's you I want, Marcus. Only you.'

The helicopter was moving again. It was almost directly overhead. Ellie dipped her head and groaned aloud. This wasn't going to work. She couldn't lie convincingly enough. But then she raised her face and saw Marcus running towards her.

Empty-handed.

The spotlight from the helicopter came on again and the terror that Marcus had thrown the car seat over the cliff proved unfounded. The seat was on the ground where he'd been standing. He'd simply abandoned it.

'You *bastard*.' All that terror and an unholy fury that someone could frighten her that much went into the shove Ellie gave Marcus as he reached out to grab her. He stumbled backwards, stepped onto a rock and fell hard.

Ellie ran. Not towards the relative safety of the lighthouse but back towards the cliff. She reached the car seat. The safety-belt mechanism was open and there was nothing to slow her from grabbing her baby with both hands and clutching her to her breasts. But, just as swiftly, Marcus was getting back onto his feet.

The roar of the hovering helicopter filled her head. The spotlight was almost blinding her. Could she really see what she thought she was seeing?

Three dark shapes well away from the shadows of the lighthouse. Moving at astonishing speed towards Marcus. And further away, flashing blue and red lights. So many of them. Emergency vehicles speeding along the road towards this scene.

The knowledge that somehow Max had followed her here and was trying to protect her was unbelievable but maybe he was too late. Everybody was too late. Marcus was on his feet, his face so twisted with fury it was virtually unrecognisable. He was launching himself in her direction. Screaming words that were incomprehensible. He wasn't going to stop. He was going to send them all over the cliff.

Ellie curled herself over the precious bundle in her arms. Curled herself so forcefully she rolled forward, landing on her shoulder and then her back. She felt the impact of a foot on her thigh and then saw Marcus tumble to land on her other side. She heard the thump of his body land and then he rolled again, unable to slow the momentum he'd built up. Another roll and then he vanished. She heard an unearthly scream that got drowned by the whine of an aircraft engine being shut down after landing.

The moment that sound began to fade she could hear the sound of the voice she loved the most.

'*Ellie*. My God, Ellie, are you all right?'

CHAPTER ELEVEN

IT WAS over.

The car park was crowded with emergency vehicles. Police cars and vans. Ambulances. Even a fire engine had been dispatched.

The police had been less than impressed by the way the three doctors had taken off after Ellie by themselves. Detective Inspector Jack Davidson was having words with Max while his deputies took statements from Rick and Jet somewhere else.

'Just what the hell did you think you were *doing*, exactly? What do you guys think you are? Doctors or members of some elite SAS branch?'

'Jet's actually done a lot of work with the SAS.' Max was trying to see past the solid figure of the detective. Into the back of the ambulance where he knew Ellie was. With Mouse. He'd had no time to do more than make sure neither of them had any obvious physical injuries before others had begun arriving and taking over this scene.

The helicopter was lifting off again. This time its spotlight would be used to locate Marcus Jones. Surviving the fall was an impossibility, but someone would have to be winched down to recover the body if it hadn't made it as far as the ocean.

Marcus Jones was gone. Ellie was safe.

It was over.

She would no longer need his protection.

She hadn't wanted it at the end, anyway, had she? She'd chosen to come here alone. She must have been scared stiff but she still hadn't included him.

That hurt. Enough to make him angry. Or sad. Or…*something* that was powerful enough to feel like it was eating him up inside.

Detective Inspector Davidson wasn't helping.

'You could all be charged, you know that?

Interfering with police operations is a serious offence.'

Rick walked towards them, Jet by his side. 'You done yet?' he queried.

'Yes,' Max said.

'No,' Jack Davidson said. 'Not by a long shot.'

Jet stared at him. 'What's the problem? Case solved. Victims are uninjured. You'll get the credit. You wouldn't have been anywhere near here if I hadn't called it in.' He shoved his hands into the pockets of his leather jacket. 'Bloody cold, isn't it? Don't s'pose there's any coffee to be had?'

Max had more important things on *his* mind. 'I'm going to see how Ellie's getting on,' he muttered.

He put his own hands in his pockets and hunched his shoulders against the wind. It was only a short walk to the ambulance but he was flanked by Rick and Jet.

'Hey…' Rick gave his upper arm a friendly

thump. 'Cheer up. It's all sorted. The weasel won't be bothering anybody ever again.'

'Yeah…' Jet sounded just as cheerful. 'Your work is done. Life, as we know it, can resume.'

Rick was nodding. 'Did I ever get round to telling you he offered to marry Ellie?'

'What?' Clearly, Jet hadn't caught up on that titbit. He shook his head in disbelief but then he grinned. 'Every cloud has a silver lining, man. You don't have to even *think* about getting married or being some kind of stand-in daddy now. How good is that?'

The voices had been carried on the wind through a back door that was slightly ajar and Ellie had had no choice other than to overhear the end of that exchange.

She'd been crying. Trying to get her baby to feed, which would be the best way to warm her up, but Mouse was having none of it. She was wrapped in several blankets but was still making that odd, plaintive whimpering that was quiet enough to frighten Ellie.

She still hadn't processed everything that had just happened. She wouldn't believe that Marcus was actually dead and no longer a threat until someone proved it to her. She was cold and still afraid and…despite the attention of all the capable professionals around her…she was lonely.

Hearing Rick and Jet celebrating the fact that the trouble was over and that she had no further claim of any kind on Max pushed her misery to the point where her tears dried up. She probably seemed quite calm by the time Max climbed into the back of the ambulance and sat on the stretcher beside her.

'You OK?'

'I'm…OK.'

'What about Mouse?'

'She's not hurt but she's very cold. She won't feed…' Ellie's voice cracked. She wanted to say she didn't know what to do and she was scared but that would just be asking for help all over again, wouldn't it? Max wouldn't want that. He was free now. His best friends thought that was a silver lining to the cloud she had generated by coming into his life. Max probably agreed with them.

'We'll get going,' a paramedic decided. 'Get her into the emergency department where they've got all the gear to get her properly warmed up.'

'You tried the kangaroo thing?' Max had caught Ellie's gaze and was holding it with an odd intensity.

'I'm cold, too. It might make things worse and I couldn't give her to someone she doesn't know.'

'She knows me,' Max said softly. 'Can I try? I'm as warm as toast in here.' He unzipped his leather jacket and smiled at Ellie.

He *was* warm. Ellie could feel his body heat from where she was sitting. She could *see* it in his smile. He had such a warm heart, this man.

She loved him so much.

Enough to trust him with her precious baby.

'What do we do?'

'Undress her. Down to her nappy.'

'What?' A junior ambulance officer sounded horrified. 'She's hypothermic.'

'Out,' Max ordered. 'I'm an emergency department specialist and I'm taking over treatment of this patient for now. Crank the heater up, shut all the doors and go away for a while. Thank you,' he added politely.

Ellie undressed Mouse. She heard doors opening and then slamming shut, more than once. It wasn't until she looked up to see if Max was ready for Mouse that she realised Rick and Jet had climbed inside. Jet sat in the driver's seat and Rick was in the front passenger seat but they were both sitting sideways so they could see what was happening in the back of the vehicle.

Max had been wearing a work shirt under his leather jacket today and he unbuttoned it. He took Mouse from Ellie and positioned her against his chest, tucking the shirt around the small body and then pulling his jacket over to cover everything but her face.

'I was kind of nervous the first time I did this,' he told Ellie. 'But you know what…?'

'What?'

Ellie's voice came out as a whisper. She was totally captivated by what she was seeing. This gorgeous, big man with a tiny baby nestled against his heart, wrapped up in the black leather jacket with its macho zips and buckles. He'd done this when Mouse had first entered the world but she'd never seen it.

And it was…beautiful.

'I've kind of missed it,' Max told her.

He hadn't had any idea.

It had seemed such an imposition at the time. Something he'd been obliged to do because he'd stuck his neck out and tried to protect the woman who'd landed on his doorstep in big trouble.

He'd done it and he'd been proud of his success. He'd known that a bond had been formed but, until tonight, he'd had no idea how deep it ran. Faced with the possibility of a life that didn't include Mouse or Ellie, he'd discovered just how empty it would be. Meaningless.

'Hey…I think she's stopped crying.'

'Has she?' Ellie leaned closer. Close enough for her head to be touching his shoulder. She had a blanket around her shoulders but Max saw her shiver. At least that bone-deep misery in her face lifted a little as she peered down at the tiny face against his chest. Mouse had, indeed, stopped that sad whimpering. She was snuggled in as though relishing the body heat.

Rick and Jet were leaning further into the cabin, trying to see for themselves.

'Aw…' Rick was smiling. 'Cute little mouse, isn't she?'

'Her name's Mattie,' Max said quietly.

He could feel the way his mates stilled. Without looking up, he knew they'd be exchanging a glance. Silent communication. Checking with each other whether this was acceptable, given its significance to them all.

'Max chose her name,' Ellie said nervously into the silence. 'He said…he said…'

'That it was the name I'd choose for my own child,' Max finished for her. He looked up. 'It had to be that special,' he explained to the others. 'Because…she feels like my own kid.' His smile felt very lopsided. 'Guess I fell in love.'

Rick cleared his throat. 'Saw that coming,' he muttered. 'Only I thought it'd be with the mum, not the munchkin.'

'Yes…well…there is that.' Max looked down at Ellie. 'It was. *Is*. Ellie…I love you. I don't ever want to have to face the possibility of losing you again. I don't ever want a day that you're not a part of. You *and* Mattie.'

Ellie's eyes were huge. Shining with tears that he hoped like hell were caused by joy. There'd been way too many of any other sort for her.

'I love you, too, Max. But…' Ellie's glance slid sideway. '…I heard you…talking about that silver lining. About how good it was that you didn't…'

'Have to marry you?' Max supplied. He glared

at Rick and Jet, who inched backwards. 'No. I don't *have* to marry you. But I *want* to. Those idiot friends of mine have no idea what they were making fun of but I know. I've never wanted anything as much in my entire life. Except maybe for one thing...' Max jerked his head. 'Like a bit of privacy. Would you guys like to get lost for a minute or two? There are some things a man needs to do on his own.'

'Yeah...' Rick grinned at Jet. 'Like propose. Shall we let him get on with it?'

'Don't see we've got much choice,' Jet grumbled. 'All right, I'm going.'

But he paused to look back. Not at Max but at Ellie. For a moment, he just held her gaze and then he smiled. 'Mattie's a cool name,' he said gruffly. 'Good choice.'

Ellie held her breath as the door shut, leaving them alone.

'She's doing that nose-rubbing thing,' Max said. 'I think she might be ready for something to eat.'

'I don't want her to get cold again.'

'How 'bout if you hold her and I hold *you* and keep you both warm?'

It sounded like heaven. 'Do you think your jacket's big enough?'

'My heart is,' Max told her. 'I'm going to look after you, Ellie. Both of you.'

Somehow, they managed it. Tucked against Max's chest, with Mattie in her arms and Max's arms around them both, Ellie was able to feed her baby. And it *was* heaven. She tilted her head back so that it rested under Max's shoulder and she could look up at him.

'I love you, Max. I think I have ever since you opened the door that day.'

He held her gaze. 'And I've been wanting to hold you ever since you fell into my arms. I just didn't recognise what it was all about until tonight.'

Strange how easy it was to push the trauma of the last few hours away. She'd have to deal with it all properly but not yet. Not while she was in this blissful little bubble.

'I feel so safe with you.'

'You are safe. You always will be if I have anything to do with it.' Max bent and kissed her lips gently. 'You and Mattie.' He moved his hand to stroke a thumb softly over the baby's dark spikes of hair. 'My family.' The hold around Ellie tightened. 'Marry me?'

'Of course I will. Yes. Yes and yes and—'

He kissed her again. Deeper this time and with a tenderness that melted any lingering chill she might have had after the night's events.

'Shall we buy that house? Would it make a good place to live for our family?'

'I think it would be a perfect place.'

A knock came on the back door of the ambulance. 'You OK in there?' a voice called.

Max and Ellie looked at each other. They both looked down at Mattie.

'We're good,' Max called back. He caught Ellie's gaze again and smiled. 'Aren't we?'

'Oh, yes...' Ellie smiled back through tears of joy. 'We're very, very good.'

EPILOGUE

'Oh, Ellie…you look stunning.'

'Do I?' Ellie turned a little so that she could see the row of intricate buttons running down the back of her dress, keeping the beaded bodice hugging her body and then fading into the soft folds of the gathered, silk skirt. Her hair fell loose to her bare shoulders, except for the twisted strands making a band of intricate coils that were studded with tiny, silk flowers.

She grinned. 'I do look OK, don't I?'

'Stunning.'

'Thanks, Sarah. You look amazing, too. I love that dress.'

Her bridesmaid looked down at herself. 'It's as old as the hills. A ballgown left over from a life I don't even remember any more.'

'It's perfect. As blue as that sky out there.

Now…I've got lots of leftover flowers. Let's tie a bit of your hair back and give you a matching Druid look.'

'Hmm. Not sure about that. What do you think, Josh?'

Both women looked to where a small, dark-haired boy sat on the bed, propped up against the pillows, watching the proceedings.

'Yes. You should have flowers too, Aunty Sarah. They look pretty.'

'Right. You feeling OK, hon?'

'Yeah.'

'Up to throwing a few rose petals?'

Josh made a face. 'It's a stupid thing to do.'

Ellie gave Sarah a ghost of a wink. 'Max doesn't think so,' she said casually.

'Oh…'

In the space of only a short meeting last night, Max had become Josh's hero. Ellie had seen the look of adoration creeping onto the child's face and had had to blink away tears.

Tears of sadness, because she could understand

the indescribable pain Sarah was having to deal with given the possibility of losing this child but there was joy there as well. Enormous gratitude that things had worked out as they had. Mattie was safe. She was going to grow up with Max as her father. She would look at him with that same kind of wonder before she was much older.

She was safe, too. She had nothing more to fear from Marcus Jones. She couldn't imagine ever being truly afraid again, with Max by her side.

Today she was going to make a public commitment to share the rest of her life with the man she loved. That was the most amazingly joyful prospect in itself but, like icing on the cake, there was more happiness to be found in contemplating what the future might hold for Max and herself as Mattie grew up. That she would have a whole family—the kind she had always dreamed of. That she might be joined by a brother or sister one day.

The thought of Mattie was enough to propel her towards the windows of this upstairs bedroom, as Sarah deftly twisted sections of her long blonde hair and fastened them at the back of her head. Ellie stood carefully out of sight as she peered down into the garden and then she smiled and had to blink hard again.

She would have sworn that nothing could make Max look more irresistibly sexy than his motorbike gear but the dark dress suit was the polished version of a bad boy. The other side of the coin and it was, most definitely, equally irresistible.

Especially given the small, white bundle he was holding. Three-month-old Mattie was wearing that pretty, smocked dress with the embroidered flowers that Max had given her that day, on her one-week birthday. It was still a bit big and her face was entirely hidden by the matching bonnet but it was perfect for today for all sorts of reasons.

'Is he here yet?'

'Um…no.' Ellie felt her forehead crease with a tiny pang of anxiety. If she'd known what she had learned only last night, would she have asked Sarah to be her bridesmaid? It had seemed the obvious choice. The news about Marcus had hit the papers just as Sarah and Josh had returned from the States and it had been enough to re-establish contact between them, albeit via email and phone calls while Sarah had been in Auckland. Catching up on all that had happened to both of them since they had shared a house had been enough to re-establish their friendship so, yes, she had been the obvious choice.

'You…won't say anything, will you?' she added quietly. 'Not today?'

'I promised, didn't I?' Sarah was threading the stems of the flowers into her hair. 'Besides, it's a great opportunity to meet him first. To have him meet Josh.'

'Who's going to meet me?' Josh was climbing off the bed.

He was wearing a scaled-down version of Max's suit and looked absolutely adorable. Sarah was right. This would be a perfect introduction because nobody could meet this child and be unmoved. And if what Sarah suspected was the truth then a huge amount was riding on what could happen after this meeting. A life was at stake, no less. No wonder Sarah was lost for words.

'Lots of people,' Ellie said into the short silence. 'Doctors and nurses from the new hospital that Sarah's going to be working in soon. And…and Max's friends, Jet and Rick. You know… You saw that picture of them all with their motorbikes last night.'

'Oh, yeah… Cool.' He had a real urchin grin, this kid. 'Can I have a ride on a bike?'

'Not today,' Sarah said firmly.

'Tomorrow?'

'We'll have to see.'

'That means no, doesn't it, Ellie?'

'Not necessarily.' Another sneak peek through the window showed that final arrangements were being made on the lawn. Max was standing by the flower-covered gazebo with the marriage celebrant. Rick was standing beside them and…good grief, Mattie had been given into the care of Jet. Ellie smiled.

'Is he there?' Sarah asked again.

'Who?' Josh demanded.

'The best man,' his aunt responded.

Ellie's gaze was back on Max. She hadn't re-alised she'd stepped into view until he looked up. He was seeing her a tad too soon but what did it matter? He would be seeing her every day for the rest of her life and if he always looked at her the way he was right now she would be the happiest woman on earth. For a delicious moment, she basked in that love, in the strength of the connection between them. It was time to go downstairs and into the garden of their family home. Time to tell the world just how much she loved Max McAdam.

'Oh, yes…' she murmured.

The best man was definitely there.

He was waiting for her to arrive by his side. To stay there for ever.

She took a deep breath and smiled brightly at Sarah and Josh.

'Let's go.'

* * * * *